Cop

This is a work of fiction. Similarities to real people, places, or events are entirely coincidental.

Author's Note

LIKE FREE AND DISCOUNTED BOOKS? Click the link below for more details!

[Image: IMG_2280.JPG]

Sign up for my mailing list and find out about new releases, giveaways, and more! Click Here!

Prologue: Liam

Fast cars, women, and the love of the game. Nothing else mattered. Well, not to me. I was at the peak of my abilities. When you're labeled player of the year, baller of the century, you better believe you expect the best. "You play the best, you get the best." My agent told me right when I got signed. Ever since then, I devoted my life to football.

You see, I was considered a champion in the league. High School was nothing to me. College? Even easier. I schooled those losers like it was nothing. Now I was enjoying the fruits of my reward. I was a fucking king to these people. And you better believe I was bringing my brothers to the championships. I always did.

I was 31. This wasn't my first rodeo. I knew how to play. And on that field, I was a killer. Some say that 30 is the end of a good player. Well, they haven't met me. I was older, but I still played better than the youngest players in the league.

"We're going to the fucking Super Bowl!" I screamed, fist full of beer. We had all gathered in the guesthouse. It was *the* place to go after the game to wind down and drink some beers with some of the guys. Hot women, of course, were invited there too. Yes, touching of the players was always allowed.

Jenkins, the best wide receiver we've got, leaned in and said, "We *have* to prepare for the after party, man. We need like a million women. A billion nipples. The younger the better, bro."

"Just press them against my face and I'll be fine. I'll just be over on some couch, half-wasted from all the alcohol I'll be drinking. You just gotta place one tit in each eye ball and rotate. You got that, Jenks?" Jenkins clasped his hands in approval and burst out laughing.

"Yeah, *if* we win. You have a lot of training to do" Clive Manning walked by, eyeing us cautiously. He grabbed the rest of the unopened beers and threw them in the garbage. "Don't get too cocky, boys.

We're not there yet." He was one of the defensive linemen and he was *always* serious.

"Yeah, but we will be. If we have anything to do with it, we'll fucking crush them." I said, downing the rest of my beer. "Man, I gotta find me a girl, Jenkins."

"You have a million of them, man. Just pick. They're all for the taking." He said with a childlike smile on his face. The cheerleaders had made their way into the room now. One girl in particular, some blonde babe with a g-string bikini on had made her way over to me.

"When you're right, you're right." I said, opening my arms to blonde babe #1. I had no idea what the chick's name was and I didn't really care to either.

"Hell yes. I don't need to get tied down and shit. Football is my wife. And boy is she sexy as hell!" Jenkins called out. The other guys hollered back at him in agreement.

"Well, well, well. Who do we have here? You look like you're having fun tonight." I said, eyeing her up and down. She wasn't just hot. She was on fucking fire. And the fact that she had already placed her hand on my thigh made me want to tear away at her g-string with my teeth.

"You were incredible out there." She whispered to me.

I placed my hand on her thin waist and squeezed lightly. "I know." I said, slapping her ass.

"Want to go somewhere private? How about I show you the VIP room?" I suggested. Her small perky tits were laying against my chest now.

"Wow, that sounds exclusive." She said, getting herself excited. I could feel her pussy get wet as she straddled my leg like a cowgirl.

"It is, baby. It's only for the best players in the league." I lied. It was just some room away from the other guys. Anyone had access to it really.

"Take me there. I want to see it." She smiled, giving me a weak look, as if she was already close to cumming.

I pulled her into the hall and we fell into a room where she instantly fell to her knees. She unzipped my pants as if her life depended on it and I sat back and enjoyed my blowjob. Yep, it was good to be the king.

* * *

Huge billboards overlook all of the big cities, action figures with a mock-up version of your face and body, a replica of the jersey you wear. There were girls to make your cock rock hard and there were drugs to make you brain fizzle. This was the life we led.

It wasn't pretty. I probably had over a hundred concussions by now. It wasn't perfect either, but it was *my* life. Only, I had a little secret. I came to conquer *everything*. And as soon as I did, I'd get out of the game. I'd get out, find a woman and make her mine. Eventually…

That was always the plan, anyway. Turns out, I'm not too good at leaving, even the things I hate. So if the suits above me need another win, I'll win it for them. If they give me all the alcohol I need, coupled with all the finest women in the world, I don't give a fuck. Jenkins was right. There ain't a woman out there for me, him, or any of the other players. The game is my wife. And I'm going to lay her down and give her all I got.

Liam

I open my eyes and take a quick breath before I close them again. The roar around me is deafening. It's so loud that my brain automatically has to tune it out. *That's it. Tune it out. Feel the leather in your palm, the thread between your fingers.*

I open my eyes again and suddenly everything has sped up. A 250 pound barbarian has made his way through the front lines and he's set on smashing my skull in.

"Pass it to Jenkins!" The coach is yelling at me from the sidelines. The infamous Super Bowl Championship game. He's got a lot riding on this. I'm guessing I do too. Truth be told, I'm just waiting for the after party.

I wound my arm back. The tension between my muscles and bone is astronomical. Within one second my arm is pushing through the wind at full speed and force. With a flick of the wrist, the ball leaves my hand spiraling. All eyes are on that perfect spiral. I smile, knowing nothing can touch me. I'm that good.

I drop my head down and take a look in front of me. That maniac is diving in the air. "It's already over, champ." I say with pride. But his helmet smashes into my chest and his arms wrap around my body. He knows it's over but he's gotta at least act like he's got a shot. I get it, I really do. But I can't help laughing as I hit the turf.

As soon as I'm on the ground, I rip my helmet off and push him off me. The ball is still in the air and it's almost to Jenkins' outstretched hands. Even though I'm on the field, I can just hear the announcer's anxiety. Will he catch it? He's in the end zone. Seconds left. This is the deciding factor of the championship game.

My hands are on my head, my teeth are grinding. Come on, man. Catch it. You have to. His fingers brush against the swirling leather and I can see the determination in his eyes. He's got this. He has to!

The ball fumbles into his hand and almost immediately a defensive linebacker dives into his legs. Jenkins has his hands around the ball, but he's pummeling toward the ground.

"Come the fuck on!" I find myself yelling. I threw a perfect throw. If Jenkins drops this, it's over. They'll win the game.

Jenkins drops to the floor and I witness something incredible. His arm snaps almost immediately, but his determination is something astounding. I ran up the field to get a better look. The crowd was going wild. It was incredible to witness. Sure enough, his grip is fastened tightly.

"Touchdown!" The words echoed in my ears. I fell to the turf and threw my hands in the air. Glory. All the hard work I had put in was finally paying off. The coaches ran to the field as Jenkins was carried away on a stretcher. He'll be fine. It's part of the job. He'll be traded to a better team, awarded millions and thrown into the football hall of fame. It truly was the catch of a lifetime.

All of the other players were on the field. I grabbed the trophy with Johnson, one mean tight end, and we proudly displayed it in the air as my 'brothers' pushed us onto their shoulders.

I'm not much on celebrations, but I enjoyed the rush of winning. It was why I played sports in the first place. And this was like winning the biggest thing you could win. This was like going to heaven. It was the Super Bowl for Christ sake!

I quickly jumped into the crowd, throw a kiss to the crowd, and headed into the locker room. I had done my duty. Now it was time to decompress. There was a huge party to go to.

"Liam! Liam! How are you feeling after your big win?" A reporter shoved her microphone in my face. I would have walked away if I didn't notice her legs peaking out from her dress.

"Peachy. I'm going to *fucking* Disneyland! " I spat into the camera and grabbed her ass. She looked horrified. I simply pushed the microphone down out of my face and laughed loudly to myself. Of course, the lady started crying, like I had ruined *her* day or something. Normally I would have ignored her. But today I felt a little different.

"I'm sorry if I came off like a total asshole just now." I found myself saying.

"Well you did." She said, pushing her thick brown hair away from her eyes. I reached out and helped her with her hair. I could tell this pissed her off, yet she remained completely still. She was young and drop dead gorgeous. I wanted her now. No, I needed her.

"Want to come to a party tonight?" I said, trying to get a read on her.

"With you? In your dreams." She scoffed.

"Well, if you change your mind, there's an interview that comes with it. Exclusive. With your name all over it. Plus, it'll be fun. Your choice. Here's the address." I handed her a card with the after party info on it. Exclusive information only the team and the girls knew about.

She crumpled the card in her hand and threw it on the ground. "Sorry, I don't take bribes." She was on fire. I smiled and walked away shaking my head.

She seemed, well, special I guess. But there were at least a billion special girls out there and a dozen decent cheerleaders would be waiting for me at that party. There just wasn't any point in dwelling on these things. I won the fucking Super Bowl. What else could a guy ask for?

At this point, most of the other players had made their way into the locker room. When I got in myself, I undressed and headed for the shower. "Hey Conway." A voice said behind me. Conway was my last name. "Nice throw, brother."

It was Jenkins. His arm was already in a cast. They got you in quick around here. "Shit man, nice catch! After that stunt, they'll have to put you in the hall of fame for sure. You okay? Feeling alright?" I slapped his hand and brought him in for a slight hug, pounding my fist lightly on his back.

"Yeah, I'm okay. The doc said I have to take it easy from now on." We couldn't help but laugh at the thought of that. "It's just a waiting game at this point."

"Right on, man. You're tonight's MVP. Don't you forget it. You're going to be at the party still, right?" I eyed him.

"Conway, you know I'll be there. I got dibs on the hottest chick in that room too." He said.

I laughed, shaking my head. I started to walk toward the showers. "You can have all of them. My sights are on one girl." I said.

"Oh yeah? And who's that?" He said.

"That news reporter chick." I said, whipping my towel at him. He jumped.

"Careful, now! You know how the media is."

"What can you blame me?" I laughed.

"Nah, she's fine as hell. Saw her earlier. Shouldn't be too hard a catch." He reasoned.

"Yeah well, I pulled a classic Liam Conway move on her." He rolled his eyes at me. The whole room erupted with the team hollering. I turned to them. "Ah, shut up and listen up everyone!"

The room got silent. I walked up to a bench and stood on it, holding my damp towel in my hands. "We did good out there. Shit, we did great. And, to be fair, the other guys did too. But ultimately, we played like a team. We gave them all we got. And in the end, we took it all the way home. Now, tonight is our reward. I want to see you all at that party. And you know what I want you to do?" Silence. "I want you to take it all the way home."

Laura

I came from nothing. And I mean nothing. Rural Iowa, a farming town to be exact. That's right, my father was a farmer and all my mother did was help out on the ranch while raising their 8 children. Even though I would be the first to defend it, it wasn't much of a life. So I got out as quick as I could.

I went to college. A good one. And before I knew it, I was out with my degree and a shitload of debt. The debt I didn't mind so much. You see, you can always pay off debt. But you can't pay off the unknown. If I hadn't left my home, I would have been like the rest of my family. I'm sorry to say this, but I'd be hopeless. No dream career, no nothing. I just wasn't going to live my life as a spinster milkmaid. Hell no.

There it was. My life, all laid out like a map on a table. It was all much easier than I expected. "When will you get yourself a strong man?" My mom would always ask me. But who needed a man when you had your own will and determination?

Cut to a year and a half later, and I had been working for a local news network on Channel 5. It was a big deal to some, but I was still hoping for my big break. Of course, that's when I received the call.

"Laura. How ya doing honey? Good, good. How would you like to do the Super Bowl coverage? I think you'd be great for the job." The network executive paused for me to answer.

My heart fluttered and my stomach turned inward. This was the chance of a lifetime. If I could just make this one good, it could skyrocket my career. I answered as calmly as I could, saying, "Oh my God, yes!" It was done, then and there. My career path was set in stone!

Months had passed and I worked out a series of questions I thought I might ask the winning team. Of course, deep down I was hoping Liam Conway would be the one I got to be face to face with, but any player would do.

Liam was dreamy, alpha, and completely one with himself. At least, he was when he was on the field. When he was off, it was a different story. He was in and out of relationships, getting too many DUI's, and he was constantly getting into fights with the media. So even though he was a perfect person to interview, I was slightly nervous about even getting close to him.

The day of the big game, I was a wreck. I had gone over my questions, over and over in my head. I felt ready enough. But this was my first real eye on the scene. It needed to be great. A shot of vodka or three later and I was on my couch, fairly drunk and wishing I had chosen a different career path. Maybe being a milkmaid wasn't such a bad idea after all?

I did the only thing I could do. I called my friend Katherine. She answered, "What's wrong? Why are you calling me? Aren't you supposed to be on the field in 20 minutes?"

"I'm not going." I sternly answered into the phone. It was a cry for help.

She sighed into the receiver. "Girl, you are most definitely going! I don't want to hear it. Now, what's up? You going to tell me what's wrong?"

"Listen to me!" I yelled, slurring my words. "Everything is wrong. I'm not meant for this kind of a job. I'm just some hick lady from a deadbeat farming town. I'm nothing compared to the other reporters."

"Oh, Laura. When will you realize everyone loves you? I envy you. Do you know that? No one compliments me like they do with you. They barely even look at me. But you, they love you. So here's what's going to happen. I'm going to pick you up right now, bring you coffee, and take you to the press area. You'll sober up soon enough, so you don't need to worry about that."

I interrupted her, "Katherine, I --"

But she wasn't having it. "I don't want to hear it, girl! You're going. And the whole time you're going to ask me questions to prepare for your day. In ten years you'll thank me and give me a million bucks, but for now, I need you to do this." She was honestly the best friend a girl could have asked for. I reluctantly agreed, pulling my hair back into a ponytail, and set the phone down.

She got to my place within minutes. With a couple sips of coffee, and a short pep talk, I was ready to go. She blasted her Top 40 radio and sped toward the stadium. We got there within 10 minutes. Thanks to my lucky press badge, the traffic cops waved us ahead of all the other cops. We pulled into the parking lot and I quickly jumped out. "Kill them dead!" Katherine yelled. I whispered an earnest "Thank you!" And ran to the press area.

My boss looked at me, rolling his eyes. "God, I thought you had flaked on me. Come on, I gotta get you onto the field right now!"

I muttered a sad "Sorry, Jake. So much traffic out there today." I walked out to the field and began my first big live broadcast.

"I'm Laura Alvaroy with Channel 5 News. Welcome to Super Bowl..." You get the picture.

The whole day was thrilling! I interviewed coaches, celebrities, fans, and of course tons of famous NFL players. And I was killing it too! So when I witnessed the earth-shattering end play by Liam Conway, I ran toward the locker room entrance, in an awkward attempt to cut him off.

But within twenty minutes or so, I saw him. There he was, running my way. I yelled, "Liam! Liam! How does it feel to win!" Or something along those lines. The words just came out. And when he turned to look at me, I knew he wouldn't give me a real response.

"Peachy. I'm going to fucking Disneyland." He gave me a cocky smile and had the audacity to keep standing there. He knew how angry I was. But more than that, I was heartbroken. This was my chance to get some words from one of the most famous quarterbacks of all time. Instead, he gave me a half-assed response with a curse word we couldn't even air on television.

He gave me a card and told me to go to some after party. Of course I told him no. But when he told me there would be an interview involved if I went, I felt obligated to. However, I found myself saying "no" once again. It was a useless display of pride.

Then he touched my face, running his finger down my cheek. I trembled with excitement. He smelled of leather, sweat, and cologne. A weird combination, yet it almost pushed me over the edge. Still, he was an asshole, right? He turned around and walked into the locker room, leaving me on my toes. So much for my big break.

Liam

"Stop checking out my dick and get dressed, boys! It's time to celebrate!" My words were met with sharp applauds and laughs.

"Ain't nobody checking out that thing." Jenkins replied, laughing himself.

"Alright, alright. Out of my way." I said, waving everyone away. I hopped off the bench and got changed as fast as I could. Tonight was the night to celebrate my win. Yes, my win. I'll give Jenkins some credit too, I guess.

"You ready?" I turned to him, shaking out the water from my hair.

"Ready as ever. You coming with to get the party favors, bro?" He asked me, showing me his sly smile.

"You know me, I'm always down for a ride." I said.

But as soon as I made my way out of the locker room, I was surrounded by the press. Cameras were flashing, microphones were shoved in face, and at least ten reporters were screaming questions into my ears. You know, just a typical day in the life of Liam Conway. Jenkins was pulled the opposite direction. We quickly lost each other in the scuffle.

I looked up, trying to see if the lady from Channel 5 was there, but apparently I had scared her off earlier. Shit, I thought. No worries. "Listen, I'm on my way somewhere. No questions today. Thanks!" I gave my best smile, looking "attractive" or at least trying to. Still, the crowd swarmed even more around me, practically pushing me against the wall.

A voice interjected, "Guys! Get back and give the star player some room!" It was my manager Jonathan Walker. "Thank you, everyone. Liam will be answering all your questions tomorrow at the press conference. If you have something to ask him, you can do it there. Goodnight!"

"Thanks, brother." I whispered as we snuck out of the building.

"Hey, I got some things to talk to you about." He said.

We kept walking, inching our way to the parking lot. I sighed, "You too? Seems like everyone's got something to say to me these days."

He laughed, "Yeah well, you and Jenkins are the biggest thing since cocaine. I'd hardly call that a bad thing."

"Yeah, well. I didn't get into this thing for the interviews. I got in for three things: the love of the game, the pussy, and the free drugs." I pushed the door open and walked into the breezy air.

Jonathan couldn't help but shake his head. "I feel you. But you just won the biggest football game there is. It's time you start thinking about your future."

"What, like where I want to end up next?" The question was important, I agreed. But it wasn't something I really wanted to think about next. Work, work, work. That's all the suits seemed to care about.

"Yeah, something like that. Anyway, give me a call this week. We'll meet up and have that talk." He shook my hand goodbye. I gave him a hug instead.

"See you, Jonathan." I put on my sunglasses and got into my Porsche, one of many rides I had the pleasure of owning.

I felt alive, you know? Or at least I should have. Instead, I couldn't get my mind off of one thing. The reporter from earlier. I was visualizing her legs poking out from her dress. Those stockings... She was classy. I knew I was an asshole, but that didn't mean I couldn't get her. I just hoped she would be at the party.

I disregarded my feelings and turned on my Bluetooth, dialing up Jenkins. "Where'd you go?" I asked him.

"Shit, man. That was chaotic back there. I got out though and am headed to the party with the party favors. See you there?" But just as I was about to answer, an incoming call came in.

"Damn! I gotta take this, brother. I'll see you at the party." I looked at my phone and shook my head. Cindy. My bitch of an ex-girlfriend.

"What do you want?" I answered.

"I saw you on TV." She said.

"Big deal." I responded. What was she getting at? I really didn't have time for her bullshit today.

"Well, you're being rude as hell. Why didn't you invite me to the game? You know how much I love watching you roll around on that field." She made a sound into the receiver, as if she was deriving all the pleasure in the world by talking to me again.

"I didn't invite you to the game because you're psychotic and threatened to sue me for all I'm worth. Remember? That's why we broke up, Cindy."

"Oh that? You know I was just messing with you, Liam. Besides, don't you miss me at all? Don't you miss my perfect ass? My big tits?"

I sighed. She knew my weakness. A good ass and a nice pair of tits. Still, her personality was God awful. It wasn't that hard to say no to her. "Look, I told you to leave me alone once. Why don't you ever listen?"

She giggled. "Why don't you make me listen? I saw how strong you were out on the field. How powerful you are. I've been a very bad girl, Liam."

"Cindy..." I moaned, getting tired of debating the subject every day of my adult life. "Look, I don't have a date for the party tonight. If I let you go with me this one time, will you leave me alone?" I was practically begging at this point.

There was a long pause before she answered. "Okay. Fine." She scoffed. And then changing her tone, she screamed, "I can't wait!"

I hung up the phone, annoyed as ever. If only that reporter had agreed to come, I wouldn't be in this mess.

Laura

"So are you going to go or what?" Katherine was leaning toward me at the restaraunt. She just had to know.

"I don't know." I said, truthfully. "I mean, he's kind of an asshole."

She looked at me like I was crazy. "He's the quarterback of the Dallas Cowboys. He just won the Super Bowl. What do you care if he's an asshole or not?"

I looked at my drink and swirled the straw against the ice. "I don't know..." I sighed.

"Girl, you just got out of a heavy relationship with that trash of a boyfriend. Seven years with someone is a long time. I think you need a rebound and I think you've found your man." She said.

"Katherine! Ugh, he is really hot. But he totally ruined my shot!" I yelled, yet I was smiling thinking about him.

"You're just mad because you know he's right. Those camera shots after the games are so boring." I simply stared at her. "What?" She asked.

"Alright, alright. I'm going to pretend you didn't just diss my job, and go to this party." I admitted.

"You are?" She asked, lifting one eyebrow.

"Yeah, I mean, what do I really have to lose? Worst case scenario is I get to go to a party with Liam fucking Conway!"

She giggled with excitement. "What's the best case scenario?" She asked me. I just grinned and sucked down the last of my mojito. "Oh you're bad, Laura."

"Baddest bitch in town." I winked. I looked at my phone and the time read 9:00 PM. "Shit! I have to get ready!" I yelled, jumping out my seat. "Here's 40 bucks, keep the change." I said, heart racing. I'm not sure why I was nervous. I just really wanted some time to look my best.

"Don't worry too much. He likes you. Tonight will be great." She got up and kissed my cheek, giving me a strong hug.

"I just wish you could come." I found myself saying.

"Hell no you don't. I'd get sloppy drunk and you'd regret it in an instant. Have fun tonight." She said. I hurriedly walked out of the restaurant, feeling slightly tipsy and ready for the night ahead of me. Luckily I was only a few blocks away.

When I got home, I ran upstairs to start a bath. If only my wardrobe specialist and makeup team were here to help me get ready for tonight. I ran myself a hot bath and stepped in, feeling the heat radiate up my naked body. I shivered with pleasure. There's nothing like taking a hot bath.

My whole body inched down into the water. I took a deep breath in, exhaled, and closed my eyes. I usually forgot how much stress I carried inside me. But now, I could feel it pushing past my self.

"Katherine's right." I told myself aloud. "The past year was difficult. Brad left me. He told me I was worthless. It's about time I find someone who can make me feel special, if only for a night."

I shaved my legs, making sure my body felt smooth and perfect. Maybe I was getting ahead of myself a bit. Maybe I'd show up and he wouldn't even say anything to me. Maybe he'd ignore me the whole time. Ugh, why did I even care? I decided then and there that if he was worth my time, he would fight to be near me. That's the only way I'd know I was something special.

I drained the bath, dried myself off, and went to pick out an outfit. Of course when I got to my closet, I stopped dead in my tracks. "Okay, think sexy. What would the quarterback of the Dallas Cowboys want in a woman?" I whispered to myself, biting my lower lip.

At first, I grabbed the sluttiest dress I could find. It was low cut, heavily revealing, black, and tight around my hips. Sure, it would have worked on most guys. But I knew that Liam was different. I had been watching him storm out of press conferences far too long to think he was like the rest of the guys in the locker room. He was a wild stallion, a stallion who, deep down, wanted to be tamed. I knew it.

So what did he look for in a woman? Well, I had heard about his ex-girlfriend, an ex-stripper turned well-known magazine photographer named Cindy. That whole affair ended in a flaming ball of shit. There was no way in hell he wanted another girl like her. I knew it. If anything, he wanted a normal woman, whatever that even meant. Still, I was ready to play that person if it meant having a good night with someone for once. At least, tonight I was.

After a few minutes, I found the perfect outfit. It was simple, yet sexy. A short button up shirt that cut off near the stomach, and a pair of tight jeans. Tonight I would be the perfect southern gal all Texans fantasized about.

But first, I slipped into some of my favorite lingerie. My ex, Brad, bought them for me, but now it was time to show it off to someone new. They were black and lacey, and I just knew it would be impossible for any guy to resist.

30 minutes on my hair and makeup and I was ready to go. I grabbed the card that Liam gave me at the game. It had his phone number and the address of

the party. Was I really going to go? Even after dealing with his rude behavior. I took a deep breath. Why not? He wanted me to go, right?

I took a step outside into the night and unlocked my BMW. "If he does anything to wrong me," I said aloud, "he's done. No questions asked." That was my promise to myself.

Liam

Jenkins looked at me like I was crazy. "Don't tell me that bitch is really coming." He said.

I laughed. "She's coming, man."

We walked up to the massive warehouse in front of us. The party of the fucking century, decked out in flashing neon lights, a perfect male to female ratio, and all the drugs and alcohol we could get our hands on. The bass was pumping as we made our way inside and people scrambled to be around us. The life of a football star. Perfection.

"Man, Cindy has got to be the worst human I have ever met. I'm sorry, I know she was like your ex-love and all, but she's a total bitch." He said, as we pushed our way to the VIP area.

"Yeah I know man. She cheated on me, remember? Me, of all fucking people. Trust me, I hate her more than anyone. There's a reason why I didn't walk in with her." It didn't take much time to find the rest of our crew, the best players on the Cowboys. "We'll talk about it later. Right now, I just want to enjoy my night with ya'll."

Jenkins nodded in agreement. "Well boys, cheers to that!" He yelled, holding up a bottle of vodka that he found in the middle of he table. A waitress quickly put another one down for us. Everyone, of course, cheered even though they had no idea what they were cheering for. I gave a loud yell in solidarity.

Truth was, I couldn't even enjoy myself. I kept looking around for the reporter girl and she wasn't anywhere. I should have gotten her number, but I was cocky. Shit, who could blame me? I had just won the Super Bowl for Christ sakes. Now I was paying the price for my actions. I soon felt a hand on my shoulder and heard the words, "Hey babe!"

I shuddered with fear and anger. Cindy. felt like I was going to be sick. That's how much I loathed this woman. "Cindy, glad you actually made it." I said.

"You sound excited." She said, knowing full well I didn't.

"Why don't you sit down." I said, gesturing at an open chair near Jenkins. He gave me a look that said, "What the fuck."

She pulled the chair over and sat in between us. Great. So now I couldn't even talk to my boy without leaning over this witch.

"So, do you like what I'm wearing?" She asked me, pushing her ass onto my lap. I looked her up and down and have a half-smile. Despite the fact that she might have been the devil incarnate, she looked hot as hell. She did have that going for her. She leaned in close to me and whispered, "I want you to tear every piece of fabric off of me tonight. I want you to plow me against the wall of your hotel room." She bit my ear and gave a shrill laugh.

I stayed silent. If the reporter chick didn't show up, I would let her come home with me. But that would be the last time. After that, we would be through for good. Jenkins was just sitting there, shaking his head.

In front of me was Randy Towman, one of the best defensive guards we had. He busted his ass in every game and got in a good amount of sacks. He spoke up to clear the tension. "Jenkins. Conway. You two killed it out there today. Fuck, Jenkins broke his fucking arm out there for this game!" We all started drinking pretty heavily after that. It was time to celebrate and the music was on full blast.

"Cocaine anyone?" Jenkins asked, throwing a huge bag of white powder onto the table.

"Holy shit!" Randy shouted with excitement, emphasis on the word holy. "That's what I'm talking about!"

He immediately breathed in a big line for himself and almost fell backward in his seat. "Woo-ey!" He yelled. I picked him up and slapped his back. "Your turn, brother!"

"No!" The words came out of Cindy. "It's my turn!" She selfishly announced. Everyone grumbled and looked at me. I didn't give a shit. There would be drugs waiting for me until the sun came up in the morning. There always was.

Jenkins wasn't having it though. "Hell no." He said. "I didn't break my arm to watch you steal our party favors." But Cindy had some audacity in her. There she was, already taking two lines to herself. After she finished, she took a swig of our vodka. She cackled with an unnerving amount of energy.

"It's alright guys. Let her have her fun." I said, trying to be the better man. I could tell Jenkins wanted to throw her out the front door.

"Alright, Jenkins. You're up." I said, cutting one for him. He smiled brightly and leaned over the table. "You know," he began, sucking up the drug, "I always feel like a scum bag when I do this shit." He laughed.

Randy slapped the table, "That's because you are, brother!" We all broke out into laughter.

Now, of course, it was my turn. Jenkins carefully cut me a line and I turned to inhale the whole thing. As soon as I breathed inward, I saw her. The reporter from Channel 5. I choked with surprise and blew outward. Half of the cocaine went flying.

Randy couldn't handle it. "C'mon man! Have some self control." He said. I shrugged it off and picked myself off my chair. The coke that I did inhale, made its way through my bloodstream and I felt a rush of euphoria.

Cindy, on the other hand, wasn't feeling too good. She immediately saw that I was eyeing the woman that just walked in and quickly formed a plan to keep me at the table. "Come on, babe. What's wrong? Don't you want to party with me?" She said, grabbing at my belt buckle.

I shoved her off me and said, "Just leave me alone will ya?"

Unfortunately, the girl I had been waiting for saw this and headed for the front door. "Shit!" I said aloud, and chased after her.

Laura

I walked up to the extravagant building where the party was and realized Liam Conway hadn't given me any insight as to how I would get in. I reached into the pocket of my jeans and pulled out the piece of paper the star quarterback had given me.

"Name?" The door guy asked me.

I scrambled to answer correctly. "Umm, Laura Alvaroy. Liam Conway told me to come?" I spat out.

The guy didn't even check the list. He just eyed me up and down. After a few seconds of torturous silence, he uttered those three magic words, "Go on through."

In I went, walking toward the glittery lights, the pumping music, and crazed football players and fans. There must've been 1000 women there, and somehow Liam Conway asked me of all people to come to the party. I couldn't help but smile. I was excited.

Of course, as soon as I looked up, I saw him. He was bending over a table full of drugs with some blonde around his arms. I felt the rage build inside of me followed by the familiar letdown that always comes after a sighting like that. He turned and saw me, coughed his drugs up, and walked toward me. He at least pushed the girl off of him.

"You made it!" He said, seemingly excited about me being there. Though, I could tell he was more flustered than anything else.

I gave a dull reply, "Uh. Yeah." I looked down at my feet, feeling misled.

"You want a drink?" He asked me.

"Sure." I found myself saying. "Or two."

He laughed and led me to the bar, away from the blonde woman who was staring a hole into my head. We sat down and I watched as he made a simple hand gesture to the bar tender who quickly whipped up two cocktails for us. "Cheers." He said.

"Cheers." I took a big sip and set my drink down. I still didn't know what to say. Here I was with the winning quarterback, and I didn't feel a thing.

He moved around in his seat a little. "I just wanted to say sorry for earlier. I shouldn't have been such a prick. You probably work hard at what you do and you deserve better." He said. Finally something sweet. He sounded genuine at least.

"Thanks." I muttered. "You going to give me that interview to make up for it, or am I wasting my time again?"

He seemed taken aback, as if he didn't expect me to be so set on things. "Of course. If anything, I'm a man of my word. How about tonight? After the party?"

"Tonight? Won't this thing end at like five in the morning?" I asked him. There was no way I was staying out that late. Besides, I had pretty much had it set in my mind that I wasn't going to sleep with this guy. He was already too much to handle.

"Six in the morning actually." He smiled. "But listen. I got my ex here following my every move. She's a horrible woman. How about we dance for a little and take off. I need to be away from all these people anyway. Too much celebrity shit, you know?"

I looked over to the blonde woman. She was still staring at us and from the looks of it, cocaine was all around her nostril. She looked like a wreck. "Is that her?" I asked, trying not to be too obvious.

"That's her alright. It's okay, you can point." He waved at her and smiled. I quickly knocked his hand back down.

"Oh my God!" I yelled. "You really don't care, do you?"

"About what?" He faked a dumb look.

"I don't know. Anyone or anything, it seems!" I said, with a slight smile on my face.

"Oh I care about some stuff. It's just that a lot of things bore me. Don't you ever just look around you and get bored?" He asked.

"Not really. I like my life now. My life used to be boring. Now I almost have everything I've asked for." I said proudly. "What things do you care about then, Liam?"

He lifted his eyebrows and sighed. That's a good question. A very good one. I suppose I like you." He said.

I blushed. "Me? You don't even know me." I said.

"Sure I do. You're the reporter lady from Channel 5." He said.

"Oh God. That's all you think of me as? Do you even know my name?" I shook my head.

"Kristine?" He said, knowing full well my name is not Kristine.

"Laura." I said. "My name is Laura."

He laughed. "Well, it was a good try on my part, right? I bet you don't even know my name."

I have him a silent stare and rolled my eyes. "You know, you're not a funny as you think you are." I said.

"Well I'm not much of a comedian, but I'm a hell of a dancer. Care to dance?" He winked at me.

If I had any self control I would have said no, but of course I said, "Why not?"

He quickly led me to the dance floor and, though he was on a small amount of drugs I didn't necessarily agree with, he was actually quite calm and collected. Playing out of the speakers was a slow song. He gave me a twirl and within seconds I was in his arms.

"Have I charmed you yet?" He asked me.

I gave a half-nod and smiled. "You're doing better than earlier. But I think your ex is a little angry."

We both looked over at her. She had thrown all the bottles of vodka onto the floor and was being carried out by security. "Liam! I love you!" She yelled.

He ducked his face near mine and whispered, "Oh God. How could I even date that woman? Don't even look at her. She doesn't deserve the time of day." He said. "You know, I was hoping you'd show up. Still can't believe you did."

"Well, it's like you said earlier. I work hard for what I want. And I want that interview Mr. Conway." I said as he brought me closer to him.

Liam

"I love confident women." I actually said out loud. I have to admit, I was already pretty drunk at this point and the small amount of cocaine was now wearing off.

The slower song had ended and she picked her cheek off from my shoulder, looking slightly awkward around us. "Let's leave." I said.

"What? Now?" She asked me.

"What's stopping you?" I asked, seriously wondering why it was such a big deal. Women normally killed to go home with a gig like me. With her, things were different.

She laughed. "You really want to know?"

"Yes!" I exclaimed. "I do actually."

"Well," she began, "I don't want to go because I don't want to sleep with you, and I feel like if I go I'll have to sleep with you."

Oh, well I guess there was my answer. Normally I would have pushed her aside. But something weird happened. It was if she knew I wouldn't.

"You don't have to sleep with me." I said. "I'm bored of that one night stand shit anyway. We can just...talk." I gulped. Was I really saying this? It was stupid of course, but I hoped maybe she'd want to sleep with me after getting to know me some more.

"Maybe." She acquiesced.

"All on record, of course." I added.

She looked around and took a deep breath. Jenkins was in the back corner of the room, with some other woman. Cindy was passed out on one of the couches with her eyes open, still basically staring us down. "It's now or never!" I said.

"Alright, fine. Let's go." She said hurriedly. I grabbed her hand and threw her into my arms, carrying her outside. I smashed open the doors and set her back down onto her feet. It was a chilly Dallas night and the streets were busy. After all, everyone was still celebrating the Super Bowl game.

"It's this way." I said. "We can walk."

We walked down a sidewalk on the strip. Suddenly she broke the silence, "Is it weird?" She asked me.

"Is what weird? Football?" I replied.

She shook her head. "No. But like, people knowing who you are wherever you go. I think that would be real weird. I think I'd hate it." She said so innocent and sweet.

"I think I hate it too." I laughed. "Maybe you can understand why I'm such a prick to the press, huh?"

She grabbed my arm. "I guess I get it now." She said. "We're all people though. There's got to be some kind of mutual respect, right?"

"I think we can find some kind of mutual respect. I definitely think we can do that. Between you and me." I laughed.

She pushed me lightly. "Come on!" She said.

We made our way forward, the lights around us shining brightly. We passed a strip of bars where a group of drunks were standing out front. As I passed them, one of the guys called out, "Hey! That looks like Liam Conway!" I kept walking, hoping they would shut up.

"Holy shit, that *is* Liam Conway!" His buddy said next to him.

"Fuck." I muttered under my breath. I looked over at Laura. She looked more worried than annoyed. I kept walking.

"Hey Liam, stop for a second. Talk to your fans." The first guy said.

I turned around. "Come on guys. It's late. I have to take my friend home here. If you want, I'll take a picture or sign a jersey, but I have to be heading home now." I said, feeling uneasy. These guys were clearly wasted beyond repair, and they looked angry for whatever reason.

They all burst into laughter. "Oh, so you think we want your autograph. Cute. Nah, we're all set on autographs and facebook pictures. We just wanted to exchange a few words with you. That's all." He said.

"Well, okay. But it's like I said, I have to go home. My friend is counting on me here." I said, standing in front of Laura. I didn't trust these guys one bit.

"The girl is fine, pal." He said. "Now I suggest you come talk to us." He gestured down with his eyes. In his right hand was a gun. In his friend's palm was a knife. And slowly, they surrounded us.

"No!" Laura screamed, although it came out as a rasp whisper.

"It's going to be okay." I whispered to her.

"Yes, it's going to be just fine." The clear leader of the group muttered. "Now get your hands where I can see 'em."

We both put our hands up and tried to remain as calm as we could. "What do you want from me?" I asked.

"First I want all your money. Put your wallet, your watch, and whatever else you got on the ground."

I did what he asked and put all my belongings on the ground, but Laura hesitated. "Come on. We have to do what he asks. He could shoot you."

The guy with the gun walked forward and put it close to her head. Tears ran down her cheeks. I felt like none of this would have happened if it wasn't for me. "Leave her alone!" I yelled.

"What's the matter?" He asked her. "Can't you listen to reason?"

She sat there shaking with utter and complete fear. "My ring…" She mumbled. "It belonged to my grandfather."

"Put it on the ground!" The man shouted. I looked all around us for an escape. The only weapons these guys had was the gun and the knife. If I could somehow get both of those, I could get us out of this mess fast.

"No." she said, still trembling, but courageous nonetheless. I was completely surprised. "I won't. It's one of the most important things I own."

"Just leave her alone, God dammit. I'll give you whatever you want." I said.

The man started laughing as he pointed the gun at me now. "Anything? You know, I was never a big Cowboys fan. More of a Patriots guy myself. And after the game tonight, I lost a hell of a lot of money. Now I'm broke. Might lose my fucking house. All because of you Liam Conway. I bet against you." He aimed the gun against my forehead. "Both of you. I want you to say your goodbyes."

"Don't do it!" Laura screamed.

I could see his finger curling around the trigger. He was actually serious. He was actually going to kill us. All over a lousy bet. I gestured to the door behind him. "Looks like security showed up after all." I said, trying to get him to look behind him. He took a short glance and realized the lie, strengthening his grip around the pistol. That's when everything slowed down for me.

It was just like the game. The roar of the people around me. The deafening silence of concentration. I kicked upward. My boot hit his jaw, shattering the bones in an instant. He didn't stand a chance. As his gun flew up in the air, his friend tried to stab me in the gut. I jumped backwards and he missed me by an inch. I slammed my elbow down into his gut, grabbing the hand with the knife and twisting. His wrist broke and he dropped the weapon.

Time sped up again. I grabbed the gun and the knife and aimed both at their friends. "You really want to try me, motherfucker?" I asked one of them.

Well, I guess that was it. They all scrambled away like a few little girls. I wasn't trained in fighting, but I *was* trained in football, which was practically the same thing. "Come on." I said, offering my hand. "Let's get you home."

Laura

He grabbed all our things and hailed a cab. We should have done that in the first place, but a walk in the dark seemed nice enough at the time. I was still shook up. Did that really just happen? I can't believe he stood up for me like that. Liam Conway. The biggest asshole in the football world. And he just saved my life. God that would make for a good news story.

"Screw going to my place." He said in the cab. "I just want to make sure you're safe and sound. We can do that interview later."

I nodded, too stunned to really know how to answer. I told the cab driver where to go and within 20 minutes, we were at my place. "This is it." I said.

"Look, tonight was…" He began.

"Tonight was incredible." I interrupted him.

He laughed and looked awkwardly down at the ground. "I guess if you think getting a gun shoved in your face is incredible then yeah. It was perfect." I laughed with him and opened my door.

"Come on." I said. "Come up for a little bit at least. I'm feeling kind of weird after all that just happened. I need someone to protect me." It was true. I was all alone in that apartment. No one had my back. Even Katherine was essentially a lame duck. I needed a man, now more than ever. And, my God, Liam Conway just proved himself to me. He was as real as it gets.

"You sure?" He asked me.

"Yes! Pay the man and meet me upstairs!" I yelled, running inside.

"Hey! Wait!" He cried out. But I was already inside.

I made a decision then and there. I *was* going to sleep with him. And I wasn't going to guilt myself over doing it. It was like Katherine said. I needed a real man for a "rebound". Okay, so Liam was an asshole. He was also clearly in a position with a high amount of stress too. Who wouldn't be an asshole?

I quickly unbuttoned my shirt and zipped down my jeans. Underneath was my nicest pair of black lingerie, begging to be ripped off by an alpha of the highest order. I threw my clothes in the corner and placed my body on the bed, curling my legs behind me.

"I'm upstairs!" I said, once I heard the front door open. His heavy footsteps made their way to my room and suddenly he was twisting the door open. I could feel my heart racing as he made his way into the room. The lights were off and he stumbled inside.

"Hello, hero." I smiled.

He simply stared at me and his jaw dropped. "Holy. Shit." He muttered. "Well, hello." He unbuttoned his shirt and took off his boots. He slowly got onto the bed, shirtless and completely sexy. On his chest was a tattoo, black and shiny. His abs were, on the scale of 1-10, a perfect 11. In other words, he was insanely hot.

"Come here." I moaned, teasing him. I ran my hands across his chest until I found his belt buckle. I undid the leather belt, pulling it through each loop and bent over for him. "You were so breathtaking back there. I almost thought you were a different person." I said.

He tilted his head back and sighed loudly. "That guy back there. That's who I am. I put up a guard for most people. I don't want them to see the true me. But you… I want you to see me for who I really am. My brown eyed girl."

That turned me on more than ever. "I *am* your brown eyed girl. For tonight at least." I smiled and unzipped his pants slowly. I pulled them down, revealing his briefs and a huge package underneath.

I looked up wide-eyed and he moaned, "Like what you see?"

I pulled his briefs down and his shiny, tan cock bounced out from underneath the fabric. He was rock hard and ready for me. "Now I do." I said.

"Oh baby…" He moaned, closing his eyes.

"You saved my life back there. I'm going to make you the happiest guy on the planet."

I grabbed his massive cock and wrapped my lips around his glistening head. He moaned loudly and ran his hands through my thick hair. I stroked his flesh as I swirled my tongue, making sure he felt as perfect as he could. I wanted to give him everything now.

"God, you're incredible." He said, staring into my eyes.

I pushed him deeper inside my mouth, feeling him expand with each gag. In and out, he pushed deeper and deeper. After some time, he pulled out his thickening member and began stroking himself. "My turn to please you." He said.

As if he wasn't already the hottest guy on the planet, he picked me up and bent down underneath me, placing my soaking wet pussy on his face. He began sucking on the outside, telling me how good I tasted, how I was the best he's ever had. Who knows if it was true, but I believed him.

His tongue swirled against my outer lips, sliding across my clit. I closed my eyes and clenched down on his back and head, pushing him forward onto me. Finally, his tongue swirled inside and out and he began sucking on my clit as he inserted two strong fingers. He curled them against my g-spot, pressing them in and out as he sucked and sucked. He was a fucking pro and within one minute, I could feel the pressure building inside of me. I was going to cum. The star quarterback of the Dallas Cowboys was going to make me cum.

"Yes!" I moaned. "Oh God, yes! You're going to make me cum."

"Mmm…"

He moved faster and faster as I held him as close to me as I could. The sharp tingling sensation made its way through my body until it felt like it "broke through" a certain barrier. My whole body then started shaking, like seismic tremors. "Holy shit!" I screamed. "I'm cumming! Yes!" He didn't let me go, he just kept working me until I lost all control. I closed my eyes and rolled on the bed, his head between my legs. I was powerless. I was full of pleasure. I was in ecstasy.

"You're perfect." I laughed as he leaned above me, ready to fuck the life out of me.

"No. You are. And I want to ruin you." He winked.

"Please, Liam. Make me shiver." I moaned.

He pushed me onto my knees and I arched my back entirely for him. He ran his hand across my spine and pushed himself inside of me. His cock pressed against my walls. I was incredibly wet for him. He felt unbelievable.

"Fuck." He groaned, pushing hard and slow against me. He reached forward and felt my full breasts. His chest was against my back. His warmth was all around me. He grabbed my hips and thrust like a stallion. His hands made their way to my smooth creamy thighs.

He announced, "I want to see your face as I make love to you."

"Yes!" I wailed, feeling his head push against my g-spot.

He flipped me onto my back and stared into my eyes. "God you're beautiful." He said, kissing me and tugging on my lips. With one hand he began lightly massaging my clit and with the other he fed me his fingers.

He slid his cock back inside of me and I said, "I want you to cum inside of me."

He smiled and asked, "Isn't it a risk?"

"No, I'm on birth control. I want to feel your cum fill me up, baby. Am I really your brown eyed girl?" I asked him again.

"Yes you are, baby. Okay. I'll do anything you ask." He said, thrusting faster now.

He put his arms around me and pulled me close to his chest. His breathing quickened and his moaning grew louder. He was more out of control than ever. "Cum for me baby." I groaned, feeling his massive cock pulsate inside of me. "Win for me."

"Yeah? You want me to take it all the way home for you?" He cried out.

"More than anything in the world. I need it so fucking bad." I said, dragging my fingernails across his back.

His body grew stiff. His eyes were wide, knowing he was about to lose himself to me. "I'm going to cum!" He announced. My cries grew louder in anticipation of it all. "Fuck!" He yelled, and I could feel his head thicken with pleasure. "I'm cumming!"

And with his cries came his thick cum, shooting inside of me. The pressure filled me up and he slowly slid back out from me. "Fuck…" He moaned, shivering with gratification. I leaned forward and kissed his beautiful chest.

Liam

"God, I think I like you." I laughed, kissing her. Her tongue wrapped around mine and pulled forward. I grabbed her breast one last time and fell back into the bed's comfort. "It's never been that good with anyone else." I admitted.

"Never?" She asked me. "I highly doubt that."

"Yeah, well, it's the truth. It's always been pretty boring. Don't get me wrong. There's a lot of girls to choose from. I've always relished in that fact. But, damn, do you stand out." I said, putting my hands behind my head.

"Well, thanks. I guess." She managed to say. I wasn't sure if what I just said was a compliment or not, but I'm glad she decided not to press the issue. "I'll admit it. You're pretty good at eating pussy. You know, for a jock." She said.

"What's *that* supposed to mean?" I asked.

"You know, jocks are selfish people. They normally don't do that kind of stuff." She shrugged.

"I guess you're right. I have an image to uphold though." I joked. "No, for real. I could eat you for dinner every night." I licked my lips.

She smiled and bit her bottom lip. "So, you leaving soon?" She asked me.

"Only if you want me too. I was hoping I could stay for a while. You still have to get that interview from me." I said, moving closer to her.

She squinted in thought for a second. "You can stay. I'd like that actually."

"Good."

"But let's save the interview for a later date. I don't have my camera with me and I'd rather it be more professional. Let's just hope you can win more games for the team." She laughed.

"Ugh, sports." I shook my head. "The whole thing is such a joke, you know?"

She looked surprised by my words. "I'm not a huge fan. But people seem to really like it. You make them think they're fighting for something real."

"That's exactly my point! It's all a circus. Like, I know I'm good. But it doesn't really mean anything. The world needs to rally behind some better issues, you know?"

"I do." She said, staring into my eyes. "So what are you going to do? I mean, if you aren't going to stay in football forever."

"I'm just talking out of my ass. What'll happen next is I'll get traded to another team, get offered more money, more commercials, more advertisement and other bullshit. And I'll have to move to the other end of the country. That's best case scenario. It's just a lot of pressure for one person." I looked away. "I'm sorry if I'm going off, but there's not really that many people I can talk to about this sort of thing."

She smiled, "It's okay. I like it. But what about Cindy? You were together for a long time, right?"

I put my hands on my forehead and sighed loudly. "God, that was a mistake. Cindy is…trouble. You probably know the whole deal. She threatened to sue me for Christ sake. I'm sorry, but that's not love. That's something entirely different."

"That's celebrity life, right?" She parted her hair out of her eyes.

"I guess so. I'm just so over that. Here's the real deal. I'll make a ton of money. I'll save it. And I'll quit in five years time. That way I can start a family. I can have everything I want and I won't have to work ever again." I was thinking aloud. It sounded like a dream though.

"Or you'll get injured. Then what?" Women always find a way to open your eyes.

"I don't know. I guess I always thought I was above that. I hope to God I am. Shit, I just wish I could spend more time with you. I like this. I like it a lot." I admitted. This was probably the first time I contemplated leaving my life for a woman. It was crazy talk. Even though I knew I couldn't, the thought kept flashing in my mind. *What if?*

Yeah, me too. Guess that's the reality, huh? You've got a lot on your plate. So do I." She said, looking away slightly.

"Yeah…" I muttered.

"How 'bout you visit me. Once a month, here in Dallas." She said, eyes lighting up.

"Shit, I'll visit you more than that if I can!" I said.

"You know where I am." She said. "And you know my name right?"

"Laura. Never got that last name from you."

"It's Alvaroy. Channel 5 News." She blushed.

"Nice to meet you Laura Alvaroy. I'm Liam Conway." We shook each other's hand and went to kissing again. Before I knew it, we were under the sheets for one more go.

It was odd to feel this at home with someone, the day you met them. I had heard of this happening to people, but in my profession it just never occurred. I was too high profile. People always wanted something from me. Now I had finally met someone who didn't give a fuck about what I did. In fact, I was pretty sure she had never watched a game of football in her life. Like ever.

She was perfect, like a flower. Reserved, yet completely confident in herself. I knew she had a past to talk about. I knew someday I would crack that egg. For now, however, I was just enjoying looking into her eyes and experiencing her soul.

Halfway through the night, my phone woke me up. It was Jonathan Walker. "Morning Sunshine. Have fun at the party? Meet me at my office at seven AM. I have some paperwork I need to go over with you."

I forced open my eyes and checked the time. It was five. "Shit…" I moaned. I turned over and looked at Laura. Her eyes were open.

"You have to go?" She asked me.

I nodded. "Sorry. They always have me going in for meetings. It's my manager."

"It's okay. Have fun." She said, slightly shutting her eyes.

"Wait, put your number in my phone. You never know when they're going to put me in a plane or something."

"Good idea." She smiled and squinted at my phone screen. She typed the number in and put "Laura" with a heart next to it.

"Cute. I'll call you later." I whispered. I got myself dressed, kissed her on the cheek, and walked out into the morning day.

Laura

I woke up alone the next morning. The scent of his cologne stayed on his pillow and I couldn't help but breathe it in. Did last night really happen? Did The Cowboys' quarterback really just fall for *me*? It must have been a dream.

But it wasn't. It was real and it was exciting to go over in my head. God, he was a good lover too! It seemed like something out of a movie. I smiled and walked into the bathroom to brush my teeth.

I grabbed my toothbrush and fumbled for the toothpaste, as the lights in the bathroom were too bright for me to see against yet. My hand hit something plastic and compact. My birth control pills.

I dropped my toothbrush and fell against the counter. My heart sank. I had forgotten to take them the past two days! "Shit!" I yelled, slamming my hands against my head. "You got to be kidding me."

It's alright, I told myself. *These things happen all the time. You're not going to be pregnant. It's hard for women to get pregnant, especially during one-night stands.* Still, I called Katherine for support.

"That's what you're freaking out about?" She asked me. "Girl, you're fine. I've spent the night with like five different guys this past month. You don't see me walking around with a baby in my belly, do you?"

I choked on my water. "Okay, first of all, gross. Second of all, you never know. Maybe I'm really fertile."

"Don't judge me for my wonderful choices." She fired back. "You've been taking the pill for like two years, right? I highly doubt you're more fertile than me. If you're so worried, why don't you get the Plan B?"

I sighed. "Because that stuff ruins your system. Some women can't even have kids after taking just one!"

"Yeah, well. What a world, huh?" She laughed.

I placed my butt on my tile bathroom floor. "What a world." I sighed too. "Alright, thanks for talking to me. I'm going to get ready and go to work. I'm already running late."

"Bye babe." She gave a loud kissing noise into the receiver and hung up the phone.

I had no time to think about this anymore. I took a shower, got ready, and sped to work.

"You're late." My boss said. "Again."

"What else is new?" I said sarcastically.

"Right." She shook her head. "Well, I have some good news to tell you."

"What?" My eyes lit up and I tried to keep my smile under wraps. Was this a promotion?

"The network *loved* the footage you got of Liam Conway yesterday." She said, closing her hands together in excitement.

"What? The footage of him cussing and acting like a jerk?" I asked, standing in disbelief.

"Yes!" She squealed.

"Okay…" I muttered. "So what do they want with me?" I asked her.

"Well, they want to send you to California. Los Angeles actually. They want you interviewing the stars on the red carpet. They want to give you your own segment, Laura!"

My jaw dropped. "Are you kidding me? The red carpet? *The* red carpet?! I'm sorry, but this is such a shock. I don't know what to say."

"You say yes!" She screamed. "You have to!"

"Give me time to think about it, okay?" I asked.

She huffed and puffed a little, and reluctantly agreed. I took a deep breath and smiled to myself. I really did it. I made the cut. I walked into my office and shut the door. In my bottom drawer was a bottle of bourbon. I poured myself a glass to celebrate. "To you." I said out loud. I took a sip and closed my eyes.

24 months later...

I opened my eyes to the view of a lifetime, but everything had changed. I was in Los Angeles, the city of angels, and my life had seemed to be thrown to the wolves. Don't get me wrong, I'm grateful for everything. It's just sometimes hard to see the light on some things. For God's sake, the network made me change my last name to something more "fitting."

Alright, time to fake a smile. "Hi, I'm Laura Perkins and tonight we're celebrating the stars! It's fashion night at the Red Carpet!" Cue the fake applause, spin the cameras to generate excitement, and smile, smile, smile!

The new show, however, was doing great. I had finally found a home in what I do. And even though my father wished I was back in the rural countryside, he knew I was following something big and supported me all the way. I still don't know if it is true or not, but he told me he watched my show every week.

"Here we have Brad Pitt. Oh my God, yes *the* Brad Pitt! Let's ask him what he's wearing tonight. Oh, Brad! Over here!" I paraded myself around the many red carpets of the world, in an attempt to ask superficial questions. Questions such as "What're you wearing tonight?" and "Are the divorce rumors true? Are you really fighting over your child?"

It was a difficult job. Even more so, it was hard to keep your sanity doing this kind of thing. Here I was, a farm girl, asking multi millionaire chameleons questions. Growing up I always thought I'd be an investigative journalist. Turns out, I became the exact opposite. Go me.

"Well," Brad said into the camera, looking as handsome as ever, "It's a simple suit, really. Pretty classy, right? It's Armani." He smiled, teeth shining against the artificial lighting. Everyone looked incredible tonight. More importantly everyone *felt* incredible. That is, except for me.

After the taping of the show, I fell into the couch. Exhausted. That was the word I would use to describe how I felt. I thought about Liam and that wonderful night. It felt like a lifetime ago. I suppose it was. I picked up my phone and searched his name in Google. It wasn't something I was proud of doing, but I wanted to know what he was up to.

I never got that call or text from him. Never, not once. And I get it, these things happen. He was a famous football player and he had a lot on his plate. But the thing that got me the most was that he said I was different. He actually lied to my face. I didn't even get the damn interview out of him.

"My brown-eyed girl." That's what he called me. Like the song. I felt so special. Now I feel so used. I vowed to never hook up with a celebrity ever again.

On the internet search, it said the same thing it always did. Liam was traded to the New England Patriots. Ironic, since it was the team he beat in the Super Bowl. That's how the industry worked I guess. So now he was somewhere in Boston or New England, or where-the-hell-ever, and I was on the other end of the country in Hollywood.

I sighed and clicked around some more. He hadn't been playing as well as he used to. The team was being criticized left and right. I couldn't help but wonder what was going on with him. *He probably feels guilty about leaving me without at least a courtesy call.* Probably not, but it's what I held onto for whatever reason.

During my nightly calls with Katherine, she would tell me to calm down, that everything was going to be just fine. "He's a douchebag." She said.

"You can't settle down with a douchebag rebound. You're better than that."

"Am I?" I asked in a sarcastic tone. "Ugh! You don't know him, Katherine. That night was something different. It was perfect, like something out of a movie." I tried to make her understand.

She made a noise of pity into the receiver. "Oh, baby girl. Movies aren't real. And neither was that night. It was a hot fling. Just leave it at that and move on with your life. You're Laura fucking Alvaroy!"

"Not anymore. Now I'm Laura Perkins." I laughed. "I guess you're right. I need to move on. It's just hard when you're young and in my situation." I said.

She agreed and said sweet things to make me feel good about myself. Eventually, I had to just swallow my pride, hang up the phone, and deal wth the reality of my life. I looked in front of me. If only Liam knew what he had done. But it was my secret to bear. Mine only.

"Alex." I smiled and kissed his cheek. "My baby boy."

He was beautiful and cute, and everything good in this world. And he was his. I held him in my arms and vowed to never let go like his father had. "Momma." He whispered with a smile on his face. I died every time I saw him. My perfect baby boy.

But situations like this happen. I didn't know I would get pregnant. No one did. Katherine thought I would be fine. It didn't happen to her, she said. So why would it happen to me? But it did, it did happen to me. I sat staring out the window, with a single tear rolling from my eye.

Liam

Everything had changed so drastically for me. The morning after the party, I had a meeting with my agents and bosses. I was quickly traded to the New England Patriots and was kept as a starting quarterback. Everyone congratulated me, told me I was the best in the world, and then proceeded to tell me what companies I would sell product for and what clothing I would be allowed to wear in public. Nikes and Wheeties. That sort of thing. It was life I chose, that much I knew. But it was getting a bit repetitive.

"If I'm the best in the world, why the fuck do I have to pander to these corporations?" I stupidly asked my manager.

"Liam. Baby. You're the best, that's why. Who else would the public listen to? They want to hear what shoes *you* wear and what cereal *you* eat. The public trusts you." He said.

I shook my head with disgust. "Yeah, well, they shouldn't. I'm a hack." I said. "No one should trust me."

"Liam, do me a favor?" He asked.

"What?"

"Don't say that shit around anybody else. It's depressing. You're the best we got you know. You need anything, you call me. I'll get you it. Whatever you want. You want girls? Boom, we'll get you some girls. You want a new house? Easy, here's a fucking house. Most people would kill to be in your position. Remember that. You want to end up on the streets with Cindy?"

I couldn't help but laugh at that last part. "Hell no!" I cried out. I leaned forward, "Look, I get it. I hear you. And you're right too. I need to shape up. I'll figure things out."

"Take a few days off, go to Mexico or something. You deserve a vacation." He said.

I took his advice. Only, I didn't go to Mexico. Nor did I go to Hawaii or anywhere tropical and nice. Instead, I went to Dallas. I retraced my steps from the night of the party. "Laura…" I sighed. She was turning into a fragment of a memory. A document of the end of my career with the Cowboys. But she was so much more to me.

I looked all over for her. I went to her place, but she had sold it. There was a family living there now. They said she moved out west, to Arizona or something. As weird as it sounds, I even searched her name on the Internet. I couldn't find anything on Laura Alvaroy. It was as if she disappeared out of nowhere.

I called her, I texted her. But apparently she had given me the wrong number. Instead of Laura, it was Maria from Wisconsin. The numbers must have got switched up. That or I wrote it down wrong. I was flustered, man. I couldn't believe it. The *one* woman I find myself into, I lose. I shouldn't have went to that meeting. They could have waited.

It went on like this for a while. Just beating myself up over bad circumstances. I shouldn't have put so much stock into it, but damn was she fine as hell. Damn did she have an ass. Damn did she exhibit pure beauty. I envisioned myself settling down with her, maybe having a kid or two when the time came. It was crazy thinking for a guy like me. Normally I just wanted sex. Girls with no substance were the picks for me. But now I couldn't think of anyone but her.

So I went back to Boston and found myself over medicating on booze. Sometimes I would stay out all night drinking. They wouldn't fire me, I told myself. I was that good. And it was true. I was still starting quarterback, still throwing enough touchdowns to keep everyone happy.

Still, I wasn't playing like I used to. There wasn't the same energy. Jenkins picked up on it. He called me all the way from California to tell me what the media had been saying about me. I was losing it. This was my last season. People liked to talk.

I had one goal on my mind. To find Laura. And if I didn't, I would never be the same man again.

Laura

I woke up to an ear-wrenching cry. It was the kind of cry that makes you believe in Hell on earth. You know, that shrill noise that says, "If you don't deal with this, the whole world will end right this second." Yeah, that was my life now.

I jumped out of my bed, glancing at the clock. It was four in the morning. "Oh, Alex..." I sighed. I ran into the other room and reached into his starry-decorated crib. "It's okay, it's okay. Mother is here." I whispered. I walked over to my rocking chair and began singing a lullaby.

"Hush little Alex, don't you cry. Momma's gonna sing you a lullaby..." I didn't know the words to the song, but it seemed to quiet him down enough. I breathed a sigh of relief, stroking his thin hair. What an angel.

When I sat him back down in his crib, all seemed well. He was fast asleep, completely unaware of the world around him. He was so peaceful. Then I walked outside the room. *WAAAAH!* Came another set of cries. "Are you kidding me?" I muttered to myself. "I have work in just two hours. Please God, just let me sleep for once!"

I ran back into the room and picked him up again. Only this time the song didn't work. *Think, Laura! Think!* So I just began talking aloud. I talked about random things, trying anything I could to get him to stop crying. Nothing worked. Then I talked about Liam.

"There once was a man named Liam Conway." I began. The baby hushed right away, as if Liam Conway were the magic words. He smiled at me and made a coo'ing noise. "Liam was strong, wise, and a great leader. Mommy liked him very much and, if he had met you, I'm sure he would have fallen in love." That part made me tear up, but I went on.

"Well, Liam was a real-deal Cowboy. He got sent on a mission, right before he met your momma. He was sent to defeat a group called The Patriots. No one thought he could do it. It seemed impossible.

How could one lone Cowboy defeat a whole squadron of Patriots?" Alex made noises and began sucking on his thumb.

"That's right, my love. He was full of courage. He knew just how much it took to defeat an enemy. He wasn't scared to take on the world. Just like you, huh?" I smiled and kissed his cheek. He was asleep at this point. In fact, he was so asleep that, even when I left the room, he stayed sound asleep.

Only problem was now I was too awake to go back to bed myself. I did what I always did and made coffee and turned on the morning news. The anchor seemed thrilled. He was saying, "…and big news for sports fans out there! The New England Patriots are heading to California to battle it out against the Rams! Will Liam Conway have what it takes? Tune in this Monday to find out."

On the television were images of Liam looking triumphant and excited. They were all images of him winning. Even though he was having problems this season, the country was still on his side, banking on his comeback. This brought a smile to my face. "He's still got it. I know he does." I said aloud while drinking my coffee.

By the time I had finished cooking breakfast, cleaning the dishes, changing the baby's diaper (for the millionth time), I was almost late for work. Even still, the babysitter wasn't here yet. "Oh God." I moaned, "I'm going to kill her! I'm honestly going to kill her!" I screamed, obviously not serious. Of course, right when I yelled it, she rang my doorbell.

"Um, sorry I'm late Mrs. Perkins. There was a lot of traffic and—" she looked as if she was about to cry, so I interrupted her.

"It's fine, Samantha. I'm sorry if you could hear me freaking out inside the house. Uh, here, come in." I waved her inside.

"It's okay." She said. "I figure it's really stressful raising a kid alone. But I hope you know how inspirational you are to me." I nearly rolled my eyes at this. Inspirational? Me? No, I was quickly becoming the dictionary definition of "a mess."

I smiled and said, "You're sweet, as always. Anyway, I'm running late for work. Here's some extra money, on top of what I pay you at the end of the month. If you or Alex need *anything* please don't hesitate to call me."

"I'm sure we'll be fine." She said.

She was so calm and I was just some spazzy mother now. What had I become? "Yes, but sometimes he gets fussy and—" As I was talking, I reached into my purse to find some baby formula. I dropped my purse onto the floor, spilling the formula everywhere, along with everything else inside. I fell to the floor in tears.

"Oh my God! Are you okay?" She bent down to help me with my things.

Tears were streaming from my eyes. My hands were shaking. Yep, I was a wreck. I was so distraught that I actually started laughing! I picked myself off the ground, wiped my tears away, and took a deep breath. "I'm fine." I said, remembering what the newsman said. *He's coming to California!*

That's it! I would meet him at the game! But what about the baby? I couldn't tell him. I just couldn't! No, that would have to be kept a secret. I smiled at Samantha and repeated the words: "I'm fine!" I ran out the door, jumped in my car, and fled to work.

When I finally stepped into the office, my manager and agent welcomed me in with huge smiles on their faces. "We need to talk to you." They said.

Great. What is it now? I thought to myself. From the look of their smiles, I just knew it wasn't going to be good.

Liam

I woke up, face first against the turf. I felt dizzy and confused. "What happened?" I asked Charlie Rollins, running back for the team.

"You're asking me? Shit, you got the ball and just stood there. You got sacked, brotha." He shook his head and laughed as if I was some rookie just learning the ropes.

"Liam, what the fuck man?" My coach came running onto the field. "What's going on with you? What's happening out there? You've been weird all week." He looked around at the other players, who were also shaking their heads. "Alright everyone, take ten minutes!"

"Let's take a walk." He said.

I couldn't help but feel guilty. I was doing the worst thing a man like me could do. I was letting my team down. I turned to my coach and began apologizing. "I'm sorry." I said. "I know how much you all have been counting on me. And I know you got a lot riding on us winning. Trust me, I do. I got a lot riding on it too."

"Then what's up? You can talk to me, man. I may be your coach, but we're all family here. I want you to know that. This is the Patriots. This is a brotherhood." He said.

For a second I thought about telling him how I felt. I thought about telling him about Laura, about the shitty circumstance surrounding it all. But in the end, I choked. I couldn't let him know. I wouldn't let *anyone* know. It was my pain to bear.

"I know, coach. I just haven't been getting enough sleep lately." I lied, turning back toward the other players.

"Well, it's about time you rest up. We have a big game on Monday. California, baby!" He yelled to me.

Right. Got it.

I came back to the other players and called out, "Alright, boys! Let's bring it in!" My players formed a huddle around me, waiting for some words of wisdom, as well as the next play.

"Now I know we haven't been playing as well as we should. And I know a hell of a lot of you have been blaming me for those losses. Maybe you're right. But this where the tides turn, brothers! This is where we come back and crush the opposition. Can you feel it? Can you see that trophy in your hands? We're going to take this anger all the way to the Super Bowl and back! On the count of three!" Everyone threw their hands in. "One-two-three, Patriots!"

* * *

Off the field was different. I decided that I can wallow in the past. I could hope and I could pray to get her back, but that didn't mean she was coming back. It was time to move on as best I could. Since Jenkins wasn't around, I had found a friend in Charlie, our fastest running back and soon-to-be star on the field.

After I showered and got ready, I called him up. "Charlie. I need a night out." I said.

"Fuck man, you've been a recluse since you joined our team. You need more than a night out. Don't worry, I got just the solution."

"Good, I'll meet you outside in an hour. We'll hit the Patriots Club first. After that it's in your hands." I said.

"Roger that." He replied, hanging up the phone.

The Club was the hottest spot in Boston right now, made completely for the players. It was VIP exclusive and the only people who could get inside were those that were approved by us or the doormen. And you better believe there was all the drugs and booze a man could handle. I put on my best suit, adjusted my hair in the mirror, and walked outside. "Time to slay." I whispered with a smile.

Outside my place was a stretch hummer, ready to pick me up. The window rolled down "Ah, shit! There he is, there's that player!"

"What's up, fellas?" I said, jumping in.

Inside were Charlie and two women. Blondes with fake tits, lips, and possibly fake asses. Who could tell these days? Neon lights lit up the inside of the vehicle and Charlie had already poured everyone glasses of champagne. The women eyed me up and down, and smiled, looking pleased.

"The night's just starting!" Charlie announced. "Liam, I want you to meet Natasha and Riley. They're *huge* fans of your work." He winked, already looking pretty drunk.

Natasha had already placed her hand on my thigh and scooted close to me so that we were touching. I pushed her hand off me and scooted away. To most men she would be considered hot, despite the plastic additions. There was no denying that most sports players would love a girl like her. Not me, though. It was impossible not to compare her to Laura.

"Oh yeah?" I responded. "You like what I do?" I asked her, staring at the entrance to her dress at her smooth thighs. She bit her lip and nodded.

"I loved watching you during the Super Bowl." She said. *So did everyone else.* I thought to myself.

"Natasha was born in Russia, but she *loves* American sports. It's a, um, passion of hers." Charlie clarified.

"A passion? Really?" I asked her, taking a sip of my champagne. It was flat.

"Well," she began, "I like the players. A lot." She smiled, her tongue ran across her lips. I couldn't help but think how boring she was.

"I'm a big fan of what I do too." I smiled, feeling myself become a bit annoyed. She simply smiled, as if she wasn't listening to a word I was saying. "You're very nice." I lied. She wasn't at all what I wanted. In fact, I wanted her to leave.

The limo pulled up to the curb and we poured out into the club. Inside, the music was pumping as loud as it could get. Second-string players were acting like bigshots, pouring back shots and talking to sub par women. More than likely, they'll end up in a puddle of their own puke tomorrow morning. Within seconds, some club workers handed all of us beers.

"Cheers!" Charlie yelled loudly.

"Cheers." I mumbled.

We made our way to the dance floor, where the action was resonating. Charlie leaned in toward all of us and said, "I got you all something."

"A present?" Riley asked.

"Yes, doll. A present." Charlie smiled and winked at me. These girls were dull and I was already wanting to go home. But I owed it to my team to perk up. Before all this Laura shit, I was the man of the party. I didn't give a fuck. The world was my oyster. Now, things had changed.

Charlie opened up his hand and we all leaned in to see what he had. "I got us all some Molly." He smiled wide.

"Molly?" Riley asked her.

"Yes, honey. It's MDMA. Ecstasy. Don't worry. It's good for you." He said. I shook my head. *I gotta get out of here.* I thought to myself. "Alright, everyone. Open wide!"

He placed one pill in everyone's mouth. We all closed our eyes and swallowed. Well, at least I pretended to. I took a sip of my drink and spit out the pill into the can. Within minutes, of course, everyone was dancing hard on the dance floor. Everyone, that is, except for me.

Natasha danced over to me. "Why don't you dance with me, baby?"

"I'm not your baby." I found myself saying. She looked surprised. Luckily, I was used to being a dick to people I didn't want to be around. "Go dance with Charlie." I said. "He looks like he could use another woman."

She looked over to Charlie, who was unbuttoning his shirt with one hand and rubbing Riley's hair with the other. Apparently the drugs had kicked in for him. He turned to me and smiled, "Best night ever!" He said, looking like a maniac.

"Right." I said.

Natasha huffed and turned around, clearly pissed off at me. It was perfect, actually. This was the realization of who I was becoming. It was apparent that I needed to lay low and focus on the game. None of this rebound shit. None of the dumb parties. If I somehow found Laura, I would dedicate my life to her. But for now, it was all about the game.

I laughed as I watched them all fall into the drug. They were an embarrassing group of people. Though I respected Charlie's work on the field, he wasn't like Jenkins. He didn't have my interests in mind.

"Fuck this." I muttered to myself. I shook my head and walked right out those doors. I doubt that Charlie even noticed.

Laura

"You want me to go to New York on Monday?" I asked, flabbergasted.

"You'll have the week in New York. We have a set list of locations you'll be filming at. We'll want you to go over those during the week and become familiar with everything. On Friday is the Afleck movie premiere. This will be *huge* Laura. You ready for all this?"

My eyes widened. "Ready? Of course I'm ready. But you really need me there Monday? Can't it wait until Thursday? Or what about Wednesday?" I asked. Monday was the big Patriots game. Liam would be in town and I *had* to be at that game. I just had to.

"Monday is a definite. There's a lot of work to go over and we want you to get integrated with the city." My manager said.

"Integrated? Why does that matter so much to you guys?" I asked. Was there something they weren't telling me?

She took a deep breath, looked at my agent, and set her stuff on the table. "Okay, so we didn't want to say anything, but…"

"But what?" I interrupted. "Are you guys seriously going to keep surprising me with things?"

My agent interjected. "It's a surprise worth considering. New York City. The Big Apple! Haven't you ever pictured yourself living in the epicenter of the world?"

"I have a child. You think it's a good place to raise a kid?" I sassily replied.

My manager smiled, "It's as good as any. Little Alex will love it there. But, look. We'll understand if you say no. But the network is willing to give you your own show. A *new* show."

I sat down now. "What kind of show?" I asked.

"Whatever you want. You're our star, Laura. The ratings love you." My manager said.

"Sports, arts, entertainment. And I want a segment of investigative journalism on every show. I want to blow the lid off some things. I want it to be relevant and poignant. Shit, I can't believe I'm even considering this." I shook my head.

"Done and done. We'll even pay for your place. How does a three bedroom flat in Manhatten sound? We'll pay for the first 4 years of your stay. If your show takes off, we can talk about a raise."

"It's a deal if my yearly pay goes up." I said, loving this negotiation.

"You'll make two mil a year." My manager smiled.

"Deal." I said with a big smile on my face. "I'll see you Monday."

"Great!" They both said nearly at the same time. "Don't worry about today. The writers have everything covered. Take the rest of the day off."

They gave me my ticket to New York City and we shook hands in agreement. I made my way outside. A new show, huh? I couldn't believe it. So much had changed within a year. I had a kid, a booming career, and now I would be starting a new life in New York City.

Of course, the obvious flashed in my head. Liam was in Boston, right? That meant that he was only a couple hours away. It got me a little excited to think about, but then I remembered I would be missing the big game on Monday. *Dammit,* I thought. I wanted so badly to see him and now there would be nothing. I would have to wait even longer and who knew what kind of women he had been seeing since our night together.

Besides, when it came down to it, he wouldn't want to be with me now. I was a single mother to a beautiful angel who was more than a handful. He was the cutest ray of sunshine the world had ever seen, but I knew what football players were like. They were selfish. They didn't care about babies. If he found out about Alex, he would leave in an instant. That much I knew.

Look, I said to myself, *that night was wonderful and perfect, but that's all it was. It was a great rebound. He's not going to be your husband. He can't be a father to your child.* It was time to give up the dream.

Even though I had the day off to go back home and be with my son, I decided I needed some time to myself. I headed to my favorite park in LA to seclude myself from the rest of the world.

When I got there, I sat on the bench and tried to meditate. I was never very good at stuff like that, but I figured it was better late than never. I thought about what I really wanted in life. At first, it was a great job. Then it was security. But now I had gotten everything that I wanted and more. I had the whole world in my hands. I whispered in the wind, "I want the thing I cannot express. The one thing I am missing." Even I didn't know what that meant.

It was clear that I was restless. I sat in silence for a good thirty minutes until I heard someone calling out, "Hey! Hey! Reporter chick!" I looked up and squinted my eyes. "Yeah you! You used to be on Channel 5 News, right?"

"Channel 5 news." I said, feeling confused. Who the hell remembered me from that?

The man walked up to me. He was incredibly muscular and toned and had just apparently got done with his morning run. "You remember me?" He asked.

I didn't. "No, should I? I'm sorry, but I meet a lot of people in my line of work."

"Nah, it's okay. The name is Jenkins." He said. "I used to play ball with a guy named Liam Conway. You remember him, right?"

I shook my head in disbelief and smiled. "Uh, yeah I remember him alright." I laughed. If only he knew the situation.

"Yeah, well, long time no see. Man, Liam is going crazy without you, you know that right?"

"What?" Was I dreaming or was this really reality? Liam? Missing *me?* "Bullshit." I said.

He laughed, "Ha, fine, don't believe me then. But I'm tellin' you, he told me himself. He's losing it out there in Boston."

"If that's true, then why the hell didn't he call? I gave him my number and everything. He promised me." I said. The whole thing was starting to really piss me off. My life was incredibly hard and it was all because I had met Liam. He used me, got me pregnant, and left me in the dirt. He wasn't a stand up guy. He was just a typical dickhead.

"Beats me. I'm just tellin' you what I know. Shit, I didn't even know you lived out here. You should have hollered at me!"

"It kind of just happened on the fly. A lot has changed since the night of the Super Bowl." I said.

"Tell me about it. Never thought I'd say this, but I actually miss Texas. I don't know what it is, but Dallas just vibed with me better." He said. "Anyway, I'll leave you alone. Just thought I'd say hey."

I was still a little dazed. Liam missed me? "Yeah, it was good seeing you." I said.

He started to walk away, but turned around after a few steps. "You should come to the game on Monday. I'm sure Liam will want to see you."

I felt my heart sink as I thought about how nice that would be. I could take Alex. He could meet his father. We could be a family. But then reality sank in again. No, of course that couldn't happen. It wasn't possible and I didn't want him as Alex's father anyway. He left us to drown here. "Can't. I'm going to New York." I said. "I leave Monday morning." I shrugged.

"Ah, that's too bad. Well, I'll tell him you say hey." He said. "See you around sometime."

"Yeah, definitely." I said, waving goodbye.

Life was really crazy sometimes. Liam was coming here, just as I was leaving. Jenkins appeared out of nowhere. It just wasn't meant to be. Life must have different plans for us. Oh, well. I brushed it off as best I could and made my way home.

Liam

"Man, I don't know what's wrong with me. It's like I've lost my powers since I met that woman." I laughed into the phone receiver. I didn't talk to Jenkins much, but when I did, it felt like I was back home. "Nah, for real. She's got some weird hold on me. It's like we're connected or something."

"Look, bro. I'm telling you. I saw her in California. She's doing work out there now. But she's fucking leaving Monday morning! If only you could get to her the night before. I'm an idiot for not getting her number for you, but she didn't seem interested anymore. She's invested in her new life, you know?"

"She mention any guys? Is she seeing someone or something? I don't get it. How could you just move on like that?" I breathed in and shook it off. "The Patriots' schedule is all screwed up though. I get in Monday morning, all early and shit. Then I gotta play a game against you! I feel like I'm in an alternate reality or something."

Jenkins howled into the receiver. "Sounds fucking rough! But it ain't gonna be as rough as that game, man. We're going to dominate that field tomorrow."

"Don't hold your breath." I laughed. "So we going to party after or what?" I asked. I hadn't been in the mood to get crazy, but I figured Jenkins would make it worth while.

"You know it, man. Can't wait to celebrate with you, regardless of who wins." He said. "Shit, I have to run. Be seeing you tomorrow, brother."

"See ya." I hung up the phone and walked out of my house. Practice was in an hour and I still had some time to kill. Yet, there was nothing else I wanted to do but get back on that field. I had let my team down in so many ways. Some of them didn't even know it. But I did. Last season I was a fucking killer. That's why I had to prove myself. From here on out, I was going to be the best player the NFL had ever seen.

I got to the field and suited up. I did my stretches and ran my sprints. I imagined tomorrow's surroundings. The screaming fans. The other players around me and the ones coming to tackle the life out of me. The pressure. I had been carrying a weight in my heart for so long, and even though Laura seemed to be out of reach, I just knew things weren't as hopeless before. Just hearing Jenkins talk about her made me realize she was still within reach.

"Hike!" I yelled, grabbing the ball off the turf. I dropped back, looked left and right, and imagined one of my guys in the end zone. I threw the most perfect spiral I had probably ever thrown and it landed right in my guy's hands. Touch-fucking-down. *I'm back, baby.*

All of a sudden, I could hear the sound of clapping coming from behind me. "Bravo." A voice said. I turned around.

"Coach!" I called out. "I didn't know you were there."

"I come early every practice. The empty field helps me center myself. It brings me back to old times." He smiled. "That was a good throw. A damn good throw. Where've you been all season? We could use someone like you."

"I know, coach. I feel like I lost myself for a second. But I'm back. I can feel it, the energy I once had. It feels...*hopeful*." I admitted.

He nodded to himself and looked off into the distance. "It was a girl wasn't it?" He asked me.

The question left me stuttering. "I, uh. Yeah, I guess so. It's complicated."

He shook his head. "No it isn't. It's simple. You met a woman who changed your life. So what happened to her? Why isn't she with you, Liam?"

"It's weird, coach. We just kind of lost each other. I moved here and she moved to LA. I lost her number. I don't know. It doesn't matter much anyway. I need to man up and accept what happened, you know?"

The coach looked angry, possibly even angrier than he was at the last game. "Like hell it doesn't matter. Listen to me boy. You meet a good one, you fucking keep her. I met my wife during my 23rd game. We lost each other too. I was heartbroken, sick, and feeling just about every other bad thing you could think of, but I went searching for her and found her. Yeah, you gotta man up and play the damn game to your best potential. But that don't mean you gotta forget about her. You have to do whatever it takes, you hear me?"

I didn't expect to hear it from a coach. I expected him to tell me to get my head out of my ass, not to go after her. Maybe both options weren't so different. I nodded my head with understanding and said, "I've been taken under a lot of coach's wings and I've learned a lot. But damn did I learn a lot just now."

"Anytime, Conway. Anytime. Now get your ass in that locker room. It's time to be with the team." He spit on the field, looked at the end zone, and headed into locker room.

* * *

That practice was incredible. I mean, it was fucking life changing. Any play we made I could visualize with ease. From the get go, it was all smooth sailing. All I had to do was imagine her face and the play would come together like magic. I told myself, if you want this girl, you play for her. You play to fucking win. *Hike!*

"Good game out there, boys!" The head coach called out, standing against the bleachers. We all formed around him and the rest of the coaches, and took a knee. "I feel real confident we'll win this one. How are you all feelin'?"

We all gave a loud roar and rumbled the ground with our helmets. I couldn't help but feel the energy flood into my veins. I was born for the game. I would win this. We all would.

"Well," he started speaking again, "I'm feelin' pretty fucking good as well. Tomorrow is a big night not just because it's a game. No, it's a big night because it's the night we turn the tables. I know you got it in you. Let's kill 'em tomorrow!" We brought it in and screamed the team's name with as much fire and determination as possible.

When I got back into the locker room, however, things had changed for the worse. I opened my locker, only to find my towel had been stolen. I turned to see Charlie smiling. "Missing something?" He asked.

"Yeah, actually I am." I said. I wasn't in the mood for this kind of bullshit. We had a flight pretty soon and I wanted to get ready fast so I could decompress and tune the world out. Charlie just sniggered like a little boy.

"You want to give my towel back? Or are you just going to laugh like an asshole?" I asked him, feeling my blood begin to boil.

"Oh, an asshole, huh? Is that really what you think of me?" He held out his hand to show that he was holding my towel.

"Look man, you're *being* an asshole." I grabbed my things from my locker. That's when I noticed my wallet was missing. Of course, this only made Charlie laugh louder.

"C'mon, *man*, why don't you stop being a pussy for once?" He replied, as he threw my wallet onto the ground. Things got heated fast. He came up to face me and I simply smiled.

"What, are we not friends now?" I mocked him.

Taking my comment serious, he replied, "I guess we stopped being friends, *pal,* when you left me high and dry at the club."

I couldn't help but laugh. Was this really the big issue he was losing his shit over? "Man, relax. You're at that club almost every fucking night. What do you care that I left?"

He turned to get support from the other players, but no one was backing up. In fact, they were trying to act as if nothing was happening. It was embarrassing for him. But even more embarrassing would be if he were to actually throw a punch. I would gladly embarrass him in front of our team.

"What do I care? Seriously? We're supposed to be brothers, man! I bring you a girl, drugs, and provide you with a good time, and you leave me alone? Not cool, man. Not cool." He lightly shoved me.

"Back off, brother. You don't want any more trouble. Trust me on that. I have enough shit to think about right now." *Laura...* I clenched my fists tightly and waited for his move. Charlie was a good player and I liked him okay before this, but he had kind of a bad reputation around here. Coming from a shit team in the Midwest, he's always had something to prove. Unfortunately, that try-hard mentality made people dislike him. Not to mention, he was a total creep. Take the other night for example.

Charlie decided to follow his gut. However, that might have not been the best decision. He took a swing and I fell back, dodging his punch. "Nice try." I whispered. He regained his balance and swung again. This time, he hit me square in the jaw. Not a good idea.

I grabbed his wrist and pushed forward with all my strength, slamming him on the ground. I twisted until I could feel the tension in his bone and muscle. He screamed out in pain. I bent over him and said through my teeth. "Now, I want you to listen to me. The only reason I'm not breaking your wrist is because I need you to play a good game tomorrow. I'm taking my towel and wallet. Don't fuck with me ever again."

I turned around to an astonished team. Most of them just laughed and shook their heads at Charlie. The coach, tucked away in a corner, oddly calm and observing, made eye contact with me. I walked past him and said, "I'm not out to hurt one of my own."

"I know that." He said. "Just do me a favor. Get your girl back."

I would. I had to. If I didn't, everything would fall apart. I'd quit the game and then it wouldn't be just Charlie hating me. I started to think about how I could find her again.

Laura

I held Alex in my arms, slowly rocking him back and forth. "It's okay." I whispered to him. "Everything is okay." Beads of sweat were forming on my head. It was six in the morning and I was already completely exhausted. Who was I trying to kid. I was a terrible mother. At least, that's how it always felt. There was no one there to help me. No one there to back me up.

"It's just for a few days." I whispered to Alex, my baby boy. "Momma will be home before you know it."

"Don't worry, Mrs. Perkins. I have it all taken care of. Have fun on your trip." The sitter said. I knew I could trust her. It was just hard sometimes to let go.

Before I knew it, I was at the airport, waiting to check my bags. A woman next to me was holding her crying baby, trying her hardest to stop it from crying.

She looked as if she were about to cry herself. I knew the feeling.

"Cute." A passenger waiting in the baggage check line sarcastically said.

"He's normally not like this! I'm so, *so* sorry." The woman whimpered.

"I just hope we're not on the same flight as them." A short bald man with glasses whispered to his wife.

They didn't know what it was like, the selfish bastards. Everyday I felt as if I was going to fall over with anxiety. But I was a strong woman and that meant picking myself back up, no matter how far I fell. And as a single mother, I felt like I was teaching Alex some important life lessons in that regard. I had feeling she was too.

Still, I knew how much he would want a father someday. It was hard not to imagine him playing ball with his daddy, going on hikes and adventures, and bringing Alex to his games. I shook the images away. There wouldn't be any of that. Even though I had faith we might meet again, it had been too long to think everything would be the same since that night. Plus, I didn't even really know the man. All in all, he kind of just seemed like a jerk. Jenkins assured me on a lot of things, but it was obvious he was just being nice.

This trip was already feeling weird. Everything was telling me not to go. The signs were everywhere. Yet, I had to. My job depended on it. It was time for the next step in my career. I pushed forward through the airport and made my way past security.

Once I got through, I checked my phone for the time. "Shit!" I exclaimed. It was ten minutes till boarding time. "Cmon, Laura. You have to hurry." I muttered to myself. On the speakers above, an announcement said, "Flight 733 from Los Angeles to New York is now boarding." I held him tight and close, and ran as fast as I could to my gate.

"Excuse me, miss." A voice said behind me. I turned around and saw an airport police officer. He was sitting in a small cart. "I'm sorry, but for safety reasons we can't let you run inside the building. Here, why don't you sit down. I'll take you to your gate. The

doors will be open when you get there, don't worry."
He said

"Thank you." I whispered. "But I'm okay." I
began walking as fast as I could without this guy
yelling at me. The man simply nodded and trotted
along.

I ran and ran until I thought I could run no
more. Pretty soon I was out of sight from them.
"Please don't let me miss my flight…" I whispered.
Then, my foot clipped something on the ground and I
felt my body sway to gravity. Yes, I was falling and it
wasn't going to be pretty when I hit the ground.
However, out of nowhere, I felt a pair of hands grab
me. I looked up and nearly fainted from what I saw.

I choked back tears and gulped loudly. "Liam?"
I muttered, not knowing whether to scream at him or
kiss him.

"Holy shit. Laura?"

We stood in silence, purely staring at each
other. We didn't have to say anything. The situation
said enough.

We spoke at the same time. I said, "Why didn't you call me?"

And he said, "Your number didn't work. I called you every single day until I had to leave."

We both laughed awkwardly. "I tried to call, I promise I did." He said. "To be honest, I thought you just weren't interested anymore. Shit, I even went to your house to find you! I know that sounds crazy, but—"

I cut him off. "That doesn't sound crazy at all."

"Really?" He asked me.

I shook my head, nearly crying. "Not one bit." I said.

"I thought maybe you had forgotten about me, but Jenkins called me a couple days ago. He gave me hope I might find you, even though I heard you were moving to New York." His eyes stared into my soul. I was so mad at him for not calling. At the same time, however, maybe he was telling the truth. Maybe I had put in the wrong number. It was really early in the morning.

"Yeah. It's, uh, part of the job I guess. You understand I bet." I said. I looked behind me and saw a crowd of people running to catch their flight.

"Final boarding call for Flight 733…" I heard from the loudspeaker.

"Shit." I muttered. *Hurry, Laura. You can't let him know you have a son now. Get on that plane!*

"Is that your flight?" He asked.

"Yeah, I have to run…" I sighed. I could barely hold back my tears.

"It's okay. I get it. You better hurry." He said. "Maybe I'll run into you on the east coast or something."

I looked down. "Yeah, I'd like that. I really have to get going though."

"Alright, bye Laura Alvaroy. My brown eyed girl." He hesitated as if he was about to say something else, but then something stopped him. Maybe he felt like I didn't like him anymore. Or maybe he was really over me after all. Regardless, I couldn't stay and talk forever, no matter how much I wished he would grab me and take me to a back room. I had a flight to catch.

My brown eyed girl…

I quickly turned away, shielding my eyes. I didn't want him to see that tears had no penetrated my eyes. "Goodbye." I quickly said. And then I ran away. I ran and I didn't look back.

Liam

I had her in front of me. She was right there! And what the fuck did I do? I simply stared and stuttered like an idiot. I let her run off to catch her flight. What else was I supposed to do? Better believe I was beating myself up over it all.

After she left, I walked with my team toward the terminal exit. Charlie stared at me out of the corner of his eye, embarrassed and angry about yesterday.

I didn't have a choice. It was out of my hands. I was telling myself all sorts of things. Anything to make me feel better about losing her again. It didn't take long for me to realize something important. I got to the exit and stopped dead in my tracks.

"C'mon bro, let's go." One of the second-string players said to me.

"Just a second…" I muttered. I turned to my coach. He knew within a millisecond what was going on. He simply nodded. I dropped my things and started running faster than I had ever run before.

What was her terminal again? I asked myself. Eventually I thought of it. I was so close. I prayed to the gods above that I wouldn't miss her. Gate 19, 20, *21!* I had found it!

"Yes!" I practically screamed out loud.

I ran up to the gate doors and found that they were closed. I turned to the lady working and frantically said, "You gotta let me in there! It's important!"

She looked at me and basically laughed in my face. "I'm sorry, sir. The gates are now closed. You can talk to an agent over at the desk over there if you need another flight."

I pressed my fingers against my temples and tried to maintain my composure. That, of course, didn't last very long. "I don't need another flight! What I need is to get in those doors!"

"Well, sir. What I need from *you* is to stand back. If you don't, I will call security and they will force you out! Do you understand?" She glared at me, waiting for me to talk back. Well, she obviously didn't know who I was. I was the king of talking back, the king of getting thrown out of interviews, bars, and yes, airports too!

"No, I actually don't fucking understand!" I began yelling now. "And I think if you don't let me through right now, I'll have the NFL bring you to court because—"

"Liam!" A voice rang out behind me. It was Laura! I felt a new level of excitement and energy flow throughout my body.

I gave a sharp look at the woman working and said, "Look, I'm sorry. It's been a bad day. If you want tickets to the Patriots game, just show will call your badge and you'll get through." She looked confused as hell. I gave her my best smile and turned back around.

"I couldn't let you leave. Not yet, at least. Not without a real goodbye." I said. She stood up from her seat and faced me.

"Oh thank God!" She exclaimed.

I grabbed her waist and wrapped my strong arms around her. I looked into her eyes and told her the truest thing I could have said at the time, "I've missed you."

"I've missed you too." She said. Her eyes were shining against the synthetic fluorescent light, and I realized that, despite the odds, we had come together from our separate corners of the world. It was incredible when you really thought about it.

I leaned forward and our lips touched. That feeling – I had been waiting for it for so damn long. And now I had her, if only for a moment. Her scent enveloped me. I pulled her in even closer. Our tongues circled around each other's, and I pulled back and lightly bit her lip. Our breathing was quickening. The intensity was building to something we couldn't control.

"Follow me." I said, grabbing her hand.

"Where are we going?" She exclaimed, although laughing from the thrill of being together.

"You'll see." I said.

I walked straight until I found a door that said "Cleaning Crew." I smiled and said aloud, "There we go." I checked to see if it was locked and it wasn't. We pushed through and found ourselves in a half-empty closet full of cleaning supplies.

"We can't be in here, Liam!" She said. I loved it when she said my name.

I locked the door and said, "Do you always play by the rules?"

She looked at me, determined to spend whatever time we had, and replied, "Hell no." My kind of woman.

She kissed me this time, pressing her forehead against mine, and pulling back every so often. I ran my hands through her perfect hair and took deep breaths. I couldn't handle how I felt. "I need you. Now." I said.

"I've been waiting to hear those words from you for so long." She said, completely out of breath. "Fuck me."

I tore off her shirt as she slipped out of her yoga pants. Running my hands across her thighs and legs, grabbing her ass, I felt like a fucking king. I felt more manly than I ever felt before. She was a goddess and I was lucky enough to be chosen. God bless her tits, her ass, her body. Before she could even drop to her knees, I lifted her above my head and pinned her against the wall.

"Holy shit." She cried out with satisfaction. I spun her around and she pressed her hands on the wall, knocking everything off a shelf next to us.

"Now that I have you," I said, "I'm going to devour you."

There was no time to spare. Most likely, the whole team was on a bus, waiting for me. I didn't give a fuck. I had been waiting for this more than I had been waiting for the next Super Bowl. Damn if I wasn't gonna take this opportunity.

I licked around her edges, across her pelvic line, and all the way down to her thighs. Within seconds, I had kissed every inch of her. With her perfect ass propped in front of my face, I spread her lips apart, licking around them and pulling them with my mouth.

"Every part of you is so beautiful." I muttered, worshipping her body. I slipped two of my fingers inside her and pressed hard against her g-spot.

"Oh God." She moaned. "Yes, just like that!"

"Cum for me." I said, "I need to see you cum."

I massaged her until she was dripping wet. I kissed her cheeks and spun her around again. I wrapped my mouth around her core and licked her to completion. Her whole body started vibrating around me. I moved my fingers in and out, working them faster with each slide. My tongue was moving at an incredible speed.

Before I knew it, she was cumming. All the while, she was grabbing my hair and pulling. I whipped out my cock and started stroking myself fast.

"Yes!" She cried. "God, you're hot."

I kissed her deeply, massaged her trembling pussy, and pushed my hands upward against her tits. I cupped them and lightly pinched her nipples. I could feel the head of my cock thicken. Within seconds I burst. Her panties hung between her ankles and I shot my thick load onto the cotton.

I placed her onto her feet and smiled, both of us taking deep breaths. We kissed each other and held one another close as if this were the last time we might see each other again.

After some time, I whispered, "You missed your flight."

She shook her head and squinted her pretty brown eyes. "Ugh, I know! Work's gonna kill me." She said.

"Guess you'll just have to come to the game." I laughed.

"Guess so." She said longingly. Then she smiled and slapped my ass. "Alright, you have to hurry and catch up with everyone right? Here, let me see your phone."

She grabbed my phone out of my pocket and put her number into it. "You better actually call me this time!"

I kissed her soft cheek and said, "I'll call you tonight."

When we walked out of that closet, we were holding hands.

Laura

He let go of our intertwined hands and walked to the bus, toward the other players. His hair was unkempt, clothes disheveled, and he looked like he just fucked a stripper in the VIP room. Well, today I was his girl. We would see about tomorrow. Sure, he was willing to prove himself for a good time. But was he willing to stick around?

I kept thinking about little Alex and the incredible future that lay ahead of him. Was I willing to compromise our situation for this stranger? After all, he *was* a stranger. I had one incredible night with him. Other than that, I didn't know him and he didn't know me. If that were the case, however, what was I feeling? Why did I long for his strong body against mine? Why did I dream about his handsome face?

I kissed him goodbye and told him I would meet him after the game. "You better!" He called out. The whole team was hollering and yelling out the window at us in good fun. He ran on the bus and ducked his head out of the back window. "See you later, my brown eyed girl!" He winked. God, he was cheesy. Yet, that made him even more attractive to me. I waved goodbye and shook my head. *Liam Conway, you're a handful.* I thought to myself.

I made my way back home and called my boss. "Hey guys, I'm sorry. I didn't make my flight." I said, sounding as exhausted as possible.

"What happened? Are you okay?" She asked me.

"Long story." I lied. "I'm going to need another flight. Take it out of my pay if you need to. Afternoon would be wonderful, thanks." I smiled to myself, finally realizing the full potential of who I was to them. They needed me. I had the upper hand now.

"Wai—" I hung up the phone before they could get a word in, and I switched it off. No need for trivial things. Today is going to be a good day.

I got home and found Alex sleeping peacefully in the sitter's arms. "He's so cute." She whispered, staring at his little hands. Then she did a quick double take and said, "Oh my God! You missed your flight! What happened?"

I laughed and picked up Alex. "The best thing that could happen." I said. "I saw an old friend and accidentally missed my flight. Now I have another day to relax."

"Well, do you want me to go home? I kind of need this job…" She muttered.

"Leave? Hell no. I need you to stay. Just pretend I'm not here. I have, uh, plans for the night." I said.

"Oh! Sounds like a date! Is it a date? Please tell me it's a date!" She squealed.

I set Alex in his crib and turned to her. "It's not a date."

She was practically jumping up and down. "It is *totally* a date!"

I sighed loudly. "Okay it's a date. And it's complicated." I admitted. "Very complicated."

She played with her hair, putting it into a ponytail. "What do you mean complicated? Oh, did you meet him on one of those dating apps or something? He sounds like a real creep."

"No, no. It's not like that. He's…" I paused and tried to think about how I could explain something like this to a 20 year old woman. I figured she'd get it enough and decided to go with the full truth. "He's Alex's father."

Her jaw dropped. "What?! Who is it? Who!" She yelled.

"Calm down." I hissed at her. "I don't want to say. He's, uh, high profile I guess."

"Well, do you like him?" She asked so innocently.

I thought about that for a second. It was an obvious answer, yet full of complications. "Of course I like him. But with Alex in the picture, it makes things a little weird. To be honest, I barely even know the guy. It sounds weird saying that, but it's true. I like him a lot, but I can't let him know we have a son together. I just can't." I felt the heavy pressure rise up in my body. Tears formed in my eyes but I shook them away.

She sat down next to me on the couch and held me in her arms. "It's okay. I understand." She said softly. "Us women always get the shit end of the stick. I don't have much advice to give, but if he actually wants to be with you, then he'll have to man up and prove himself. Because as of right now, he's done nothing of the sort."

I shook my head. "It's not really *all* his fault. There's more to it." I admitted.

"Like hell it's not!" She yelled, getting fired up. "It's all his fault!"

I couldn't help but laugh. "Alright, fine. Whatever. Anyway, I'm willing to forgive him. I just don't know if I'm willing to bring Alex into this. You're right. He has to prove himself. So far, he hasn't."

"That's right! He hasn't. But he will. You have it all. He'll pine for you, girl." She said confidently.

* * *

It wasn't long before he texted me. "There's a booth with your name on it. Best seat in the house. There's a badge in there you can wear to get all the food and drinks you can handle. Go crazy, the night is yours, baby." Right after he sent me those words, he sent a picture. It was a luscious room, complete with leather couches, a stereo system, and everything else you'd want during a game.

"I'll only come if you sign my football." I said sarcastically.

"Deal. See you after the game." He said.

For the first time in a long time, I felt that feeling in my stomach. You know, the feeling of butterflies. I hadn't felt that since college. Okay, so he was trying a little bit at least. He wasn't perfect and it wasn't all his fault for not finding me. I left, gave him the wrong number, and he tried his hardest to get to me. I didn't really hold any grudges. Mainly, I was just excited to get to know the guy. We had such a strong connection, what could possibly go wrong?

From the other room came the sound of Alex's shrill cries. *Oh yeah. There's that...*

Liam

She was coming to the game. She was really coming. I honestly couldn't believe it. Most of this season I had felt like shit. It was one bad day after another. My playing was horrible out there on the field. My team resented me for it. But now was my time to make a come back. Now was the time for me to shine.

"Alright, bring it in." I said to the rest of the players before the game. "Look, I gotta level with ya'll today. It's not easy for a guy like me to lay my cards all out on the table, but it's something I feel I need to do. I've had my head in my ass this past season. I've let you all down. Charlie, I'm lookin' at you. I'm sorry, brother."

He nodded as if to say, "It's all water under the bridge."

I continued my speech, "So I get it if I'm not the most popular guy on the field. That's okay. I've never been the most liked. What I come to you with is this: my utmost apology and a guarantee for you all. I promise you that I won't fuck up again. I know how far behind we are in the stats. I know just how much we need to win to be taken serious again. But I'm tellin' you right now that we can do it. We can fucking do this and I won't let you down. Never again. You all with me?"

I looked at the small crowd of players around me. There was silence and a whole lot of hesitance in the air. Finally, after mulling it over for a few minutes, Charlie came forward.

"I'm with you, man." He said, giving me a huge man-hug.

"Thanks, brother." I said in his ear.

"Anybody else? Or is it just Charlie who's cool with me now?" I asked.

"Just don't let us down." Another player said. I nodded.

Slowly but surely, everyone stood up and said their words. They were all on my side. That is, they would be if I proved myself to the team. Well, I had a lot of proving to do, but I knew I could get it done with hard work and severe determination. Anything was in reach if I really wanted it. And God damn did I want it.

"Alright, assholes. Let's bring it in! Who are we?" I yelled.

"The motherfuckin' Patriots!" Charlie screamed.

"What did we come here to do?" I asked them, pounding my chest.

"We came to destroy!" Dalton Wiseman, a defensive lineman yelled.

"That's right! We are the destroyers! Patriots till our last dying breath. We're a united team and we will not be stopped! Today is our day, boys!"

"RAH!" Everyone cheered, banging their heads against each other, the walls, even the ground. The energy was uplifting and exciting. I felt our win already.

From the door of the locker room, we could hear the loudspeaker say, "…the New England Patriots!" This, of course was our cue. We smashed open those metal doors and lunged out into the field. We went full force, running to the starting positions. Those who weren't out on the field were on the sidelines cheering everyone on. The cheerleaders, all with bright smiles on their faces, did spins and backflips.

Our opponents, the Rams, kicked the ball toward our best players. The spinning ball of pig skin was spiraling in the air, right above my head. I looked away, up at the booth where Laura was sitting, and pointed at her. Then, I caught that ball and ran as fast and hard as I could. The crowd roared in approval, as I smashed through the defense of the other team. It was clear we were already at an insane advantage.

I found myself underneath at least three of their defensive men. "Keep on trying, boy." One of them whispered to me. "We're going to make sure you never go to the playoffs ever again." He said, laughing.

"Get off me." I said, picking myself up off the field. "I've got nothing to prove except my love of the game." I said, feeling proud.

Pretty soon, we were winning the game. And by winning, I mean by a lot. I'd like to take all the credit for it too, but I couldn't. In fact, it was the best all of our team had played during this season. Advertising agencies, sportswear, and soda companies were all most likely lining up and making calls to get us to be their spokesmen.

However, only two things were on my mind: Winning the game and winning Laura's heart. Every play I made, I would look up to that box and I would see a speck of a person looking down at me. Her beautiful hair, that incredible body. I hoped she was feeling something for me. Because I sure did feel something for her.

Halftime came and went. We were enthused. We were going to win this one. We had to. On the field, I came face to face with Jenkins. He looked kind of sour, but when I walked past him he whispered, "Keep killin' it out there, brother. Always rooting for you, no matter who you're playing against."

His camaraderie was special, that's for sure. I gave him a thumbs up and said, "Me too, Jenks. You're one of the best." No doubt the media would have a field day with that one.

Well, maybe I shouldn't have said what I said to Jenkins. Because, before I knew it, he was zipping through our defensive linemen, pushing past our linebackers and slamming that ball into the end zone.

"Fuck!" I yelled, each time he scored.

By the fourth quarter, we found ourselves in deep shit. We were down by 3, with only five minutes to spare. Was it even possible to catch up? Of course it was. But time was running out and our run this season had the whole stadium in doubts. "Will Liam Conway fail again?" Was the question on everybody's mind. Well, fuck 'em. I was in it to win it.

Our coach, sane as he was, called a quick time out. We had some strategy to go over.

"Alright," He said, "This is the time to prove yourselves. We all thought we had this one in the bag, but it turns out they have some tricks up their sleeves.

Well, so do we. And here it is." In his hand was the big play book. It was made by one of the first coaches and ever since then, it had been secretly handed down generation after generation. There were some serious plays in that book. At this point, it was looking like we needed a miracle.

"What's the play, Coach?" I asked him, spitting my mouth guard out.

"The play is called Lock and Release. Liam I'm going to have you get sacked." He said calmly.

My eyes widened. "Me? What do you want me to get sacked for? I've been playing good, haven't I?"

"Don't worry, you've been playing great. But I have an idea. We need to fake them out. Charlie, you up to play a little quarterback today?" He asked Charlie, who's expression also looked doubtful.

"I'm up for whatever you want, Coach. Just tell me what to do and I'll do it."

"Well alright then, boys. Looks like we have a play. Liam, you're going to fake quarterback. When the ball is given to you, you're going to hand it off to Charlie. The whole time you need to act like you still have the ball. They'll sack you, but by the time they do, Charlie will have passed it to Jimmy over here. Jimmy, you'll be in the end zone and you'll bring it home. Alright, you guys ready?" He asked us.

I looked at Charlie and then at Jimmy. All three nodded with confidence and clarity. "Ready as we'll ever be." I said.

"Okay, boys. Counting on all of you. I know you won't let me down."

We walked back onto the field, drenched in sweat, endorphins flooding through our body. It was now or never and the clock was ticking. We needed to get one touch down. Just one.

I looked up at the booth with Laura in it. I felt a surge of passion rush through me. "You got this." I whispered to myself, running my hands across my pads. I grabbed Charlie and Jimmy's helmets and slammed mine against theirs. "We got this!" I yelled.

I started the play. I was ready. "Blue 42! Red 64! Hut! Hut! *Hike!*" I felt that leather spin into my hands and I immediately dropped back. It slipped out of the side of my hands, falling perfectly into

Charlie's. We both dropped back. The defensive line had broken through our guards. I faked as if I were going to make a run for it. I was almost instantly sacked.

I smiled and turned my head to look through the cracks of the bodies on top of me. Charlie gave me a look and then aimed at Jimmy who was nearing the end zone. "Come on, you son of a bitch!" I yelled. "Go! Go! Go!"

Jimmy's eyes lit up as he realized the ball was spinning faster than he predicted. At this point, everyone was staring his way. Would he win the game? Or would he lose everything for us? I held my breath and hoped to God he caught it.

He ran full speed and took a sharp dive into the end zone. With outstretched arms and open hands, he turned his body and caught that glorious spinning piece of leather. The ball sunk into his chest, safe and secure as a baby held by its mother. I pushed the men off me, jumped up, and ran into the end zone to dog-pile Jimmy.

"TOUCHDOWN!" The screens flashed with neon firework-like images. The Patriots logo was everywhere, shining in full glory. We won. "We fucking won!" Charlie yelled as he joined the dog-pile.

I glanced up at the box. It was suddenly empty. Confused, I made my way off field with the other players. Instead of taking a shower, I ran out of the locker room and into the inner parts of the stadium, making my way through fans left and right. They were screaming at me, "Liam! Take a picture with me! Sign my football!"

I just kept running. Finally, I found her. She was standing outside. But instead of wearing a happy smile, she had tears in her eyes.

Laura

"I'm sorry. I'm so fucking sorry." I said, unable to hold my tears in. I was in a bind. A true fucking bind. After seeing his determination out there and watching him win that game, I kept thinking about how he was Alex's dad. There was a mixture of happiness and utter desperation in my emotions, and I didn't know what to do.

"What's the matter, baby?" He asked, running toward me. He held me and stroked my hair. "Hey, are you okay? Did I make you sad somehow?"

I shook my head. Oh, how vain men could be sometimes. "No." I said, although I guess he was mildly right when you think about it. "I'm just so happy." I mumbled, lying. I had to lie. How could I tell him I had his child a year ago? He'd be furious.

Still, I liked being around him. I liked the way he talked, the way he held me, and I especially liked the way he looked into my eyes. I used to hate football players and jocks of all kinds. Now, I was falling for the biggest jock on the planet. What was I even doing?

"Well you don't look too happy." He said.

I wiped my tears away and gave a little sniffle. "I'm okay. I promise." I took a deep breath and within a few moments I was actually fine. It's amazing what a good cry will do for you. "Don't you have to hit the showers?" I asked him.

"Nah, they don't need me anymore." He laughed. "Besides, I just want to spend this time with you."

I looked at him. He was so sly. "Can I see the locker room?" I asked, returning his sly smile. "Will the players still be in there?"

"Oh, I get it." He laughed. "You want to see all the naked players, huh?"

I shook my head and pushed him playfully, "No! I just want to see it if it's empty. I want to walk through those doors and go into the hallway where you enter the field. I want to know what that's like, that's all."

"Follow me." He said. He was still in his padding, covered in sweat and green patches from the field below. He was like a warrior, coming back from battle. He was hotter than ever, I could barely hold back from drooling.

He led me through the private doors, down the stairway, and into the locker room. It wasn't anything special, of course, but that's not why I wanted to go down there. "You look a little sweaty." I smiled. "I think you need a shower." I suggested.

"Ha, yeah I guess I do…" He muttered.

"Well, go on. Strip for me." I said, eyeing him.

"You want me to strip?" He couldn't hold back from laughing.

"It's not funny." I said. "Strip for me, Cowboy."

Without saying a word, he undid the laces of his pants and clipped out of his padding. His incredible abs were glistening with beads of perspiration. He threw off his pants and stood there in front of, fully nude. "You like what you see, honey?"

My mouth hung open. I could feel myself start to get incredibly wet. "I love it." I said.

He walked slowly over to the showers and turned one of them on. I watched him steadily as he got in it, soaping his Romanesque body. I ran my hands on my breasts, quickly dropping them between my legs. I slowly got out of my clothes and stepped in with him. He looked at me as the water fell onto both our bodies.

"Now," I began, dropping to my knees. "I think we have a little celebrating to do. Don't you agree?"

He choked. "I do. I need you to give me my trophy." He said.

"Here it is, big boy." I smiled.

He closed his eyes and I kissed his legs upward, kissing his inner thighs and pelvic muscles. Finally, I dragged my wet tongue across his huge cock, feeling every ridge of him. He slid inside my mouth, but only for a second until I pulled him back out, teasing him.

"I need you inside me. Now." I begged him. It had been so long since he had been and the pain of not having him was too much at this point. He spun me around and placed his hands on my ass, feeling every inch of my flesh. He groaned with pleasure as he grabbed his cock and entered me.

"Fuck." I moaned. "You're so much bigger than I remembered."

He kissed my back and then my neck, circling his tongue around my ear. I shivered with utter satisfaction and desire. I closed my eyes. I just wanted to feel him.

The hot water from the shower was pouring on us, as steam rose around the room. Soon enough, we could barely see each other, but I could feel as he thrust his body into mine in strong rhythmic motions.

"Yes!" I exclaimed, face against the tiled wall.

He pulled himself out from me and turned me around so that I was facing him now. "I like this game we play." He said. "But I'd like to keep playing it if you know what I mean." He kissed me, pulling back on my bottom lip.

"Are you asking me to be your girlfriend?" I asked him.

"I'm saying I like to be around you. That's all." He said.

"Be around me. I dare you."

He kissed me again and picked me up, setting me down on his cock. He pushed into me, still staring directly into my eyes, and moaned. "I think I'm going to cum already." He laughed, brushing the wet hair out of my eyes.

"Cum inside of me." I said. This time, I was a bit more careful. I wasn't as stupid with the pill as I was two years ago. "I want to feel it."

It came fast this time. He had been holding it all in, all for me he said. I felt as he thickened inside of me, pouring his life into me. I grabbed around his shoulders and pushed into him, feeling him as close and deep as he could go. His pelvic muscles pushed into me.

When it was over, he looked at me exhausted and said, "Who are you Laura Alvaroy? Where have you been hiding my whole life?"

"Oh, you know. I've been around. You just didn't look hard enough."

Liam

"Well," She said, as we got dressed again, "I guess you have to go and be with the team, huh?"

I shrugged and gave her a small nod. "Yeah, I guess so. I have some time to kill though. Can I take you home?"

She smiled and replied, "I would love that, Liam."

I had my driver pick us up. Nothing too fancy, just a rental SUV. Still, it felt good to sit next to her for the ride. There was so much I wanted to do with her now. I wanted to prove to her that I wasn't some stupid jock. I needed her to know that I was different from the rest of them. I wasn't like Charlie. If only she knew that I had been thinking about her all this time. She knew to some extent, but not the whole thing. From here on out, I was going to show her I was better than the rest.

We pulled into her driveway and parked. "Thanks Simon. It was a wonderful drive." I said to my driver. He opened the doors for us and gave a half-bow. It was a joke he liked to make with me, as if I were royalty or some shit. I laughed and said, "Okay, Okay. I'll be out in a bit." I said.

We walked up to the steps of her porch. She stopped me and asked, "Sure you can't stay for a while?" She looked down, seemingly embarrassed by the question. "It's just that we haven't gotten much time together. I'd like to get to know you better."

It wasn't a tough sell. Not one bit. "I'll stay as long as you want me to." I said. I turned to Simon, my driver, and said, "Hey, Simon! Might be a little longer than I let on."

"As long as you tip me big, I don't care." He said, with a comic smile on his face.

I shook my head. "Always emptying my pocket."

She unlocked the door, but hesitated on opening it. Inside was the sound of crying. "Sorry! I, uh. I think my, uh, sister is still here."

"You have a sister?" I asked her. "I'd love to meet her."

She began stuttering. It was actually pretty damn weird. "No, well, yes! But she's not well. She's, uh, a little sick in the head."

"Oh. Well, still. She's your sister. Anyone related to you is worth meeting." I said. "But what was that crying? Sounded like a baby or something."

"Ugh, she's always blasting that TV. Is it okay if I just go inside and check on her real quick? It'll only be one second." She said. She actually looked really worried at this point. I wondered just how bad this sister was.

She quickly opened the door and ran inside, slamming it behind her. "Damn." I whispered, feeling pretty damn confused about everything. I paced around the porch until finally Laura and her sister came outside. When they did, however, they were both looking kind of crazy.

"Took you guy gals long enough." I said, half-joking.

Her sister got up in face and pointed at me. I jumped back. "You treat her with respect, God dammit!" She said loudly. "If you don't, I swear I'll find you and it won't be pretty!"

"Okay…" I muttered. "You don't need to worry, trust me."

"Ha!" She cackled. Then she turned to Laura and whispered sweetly, "Goodnight, darling."

She walked away with a dignified smile. "What was that about?" I asked her.

"Told you she was crazy." She said. "Come in. Let's relax."

We walked inside. She sat down, but I walked in the hallway, looking at her home. It was nice. Like, really fucking nice. "Hey, come and sit down with me." She said.

"You have two bedrooms? Is the second one a study or something?" I asked her. I always wanted a second room to put a small gym in it or something. Seemed nice.

"Yes!" She said, jumping up from the couch. She ran toward me and grabbed my arm. "Come on," she pleaded, "Sit and talk with me. Do you want a beer? I'll get you a beer."

"What's wrong? Why do you want me to sit down so bad? What's going on with you?" I asked her. Something felt off, like she was hiding something from me. I just couldn't put my finger on what it was.

"Wrong? Nothing's wrong. I just like your company. I guess that's wrong of me." She was starting to get defensive. She was even a little red in the face.

I sighed. "Fine. Whatever. I'll sit down."

I sat down on the couch and faced her. "Alright, what do you want to know?" I asked her.

"Everything." She smiled. "Tell me everything."

"It's a typical American story. Father meets mother. Mother has a baby. Father leaves family because he can't handle the responsibility."

"Oh." Her eyes dropped. "I'm sorry. I didn't mean to get so personal so fast. I'm really sorry Liam."

I put my hand on her thigh. "Don't worry about it. I wouldn't have told you if I didn't trust you. It's something that happened a long time ago. It's over and done with, you know?"

"I know." She said. "Did you ever try and find him? Your dad, I mean."

"Of course I did. But my mom refused for so long. All of my wins, all of those games, I pictured his face on the other players I plowed through. I wanted to find him and kill him. I'm not ashamed to say it. He left my mother high and dry. And believe me, my mom's a fucking saint. I'd do anything for her."

I laughed suddenly and said, "I guess that's why I was always such a bastard to people in the industry. It was like everything that annoyed me was his fault somehow. Of course, that's not true at all. Eventually, you grow older and you just have to move past it."

She laughed too. "Is that a new mantra for you? I remember meeting a certain someone two years ago and them not being too nice to me."

"I'm trying to be a different man." I admitted. "Someone different than my dad."

Her eyes sparkled against the low lighting of the room. "I like that." She smiled.

"Me too." I said.

Suddenly, my phone started ringing. I looked down. It was my manager. I stared at the screen, debating whether or not I should answer. "It's one of the suits. I'll ignore him." I said. But as soon as I hit "decline" on my phone, the sound of crying came from that other room.

I turned to Laura trying to figure out what the crying was coming from. "That doesn't sound like the TV…" I mumbled.

"I…" She stuttered.

"It sounds like a child…" I said, standing up suddenly. Tears were streaming down her eyes.

I walked toward the room. I opened the door. "I'm sorry." She said, falling to her knees in tears. "I didn't want you to know."

Now I know…

Laura

"What's his name?" He said, standing over the crib. A dark shadow was cast over his face. I couldn't tell if he was angry, sad, or just confused. It didn't look or feel good. In that moment, I wished that he never even came over. It wasn't even my fault that any of this happened. It was him. It was Liam fucking Conway who neglected me and the baby.

"His name is Alex." I said, wiping the tears from my eyes. Alex looked at his father and smiled. There were no more cries coming from that crib.

"Why didn't you tell me?" He asked, leaning over the railing of the crib.

"How the *fuck* was I supposed to tell you when you ran off without any word or justification?" I was trying my damn hardest not to scream. Every organ in my body was on fire. But mainly, I just wanted to curl up into a ball and disappear forever.

He turned around with a stressed look in his eyes and said, "Me? You're blaming me for this? Look, honey, I'm not some deadbeat. I don't know what you think of me, but this here is both our mistake."

My jaw dropped. I was astonished. "Mistake?! Don't you ever call him a mistake. He is the best thing that has ever happened. God, I knew I shouldn't have seen you again! You're not trustworthy. You're just Liam Conway, the best football player in the world, mommy's golden little boy. Well, let me break something to you. You're not all that special. That baby over there is one million times more special than you. He'll probably get ten Super Bowl trophies *and* the Noble Peace Prize. That's how fucking special he is!"

Alex started to cry again. I walked up to the crib and picked him up, cradling him as gently as I could in the moment. I turned and walked out of the room. "Wait!" Liam yelled, running after me. He touched my arm and I hit his hand away.

"Just go home." I whispered. "I don't want to be near you right now."

"Just hold on for a minute. Please? Please just hear me out? Look, I know I'm an asshole. I know! But just give me a chance to explain." He said.

I set Alex down on the couch and crossed my arms, waiting for an explanation. "Go ahead." I said. "I'm waiting."

"Look, I didn't know I got you pregnant. If I did, things would be very different."

I burst out laughing, angered by his lack of foresight. "Things would be very different, huh. You mean, Alex wouldn't be here."

He shook his head with haste, "What? No. That's not what I mean at all. I mean, we could have figured this all out together." He turned and looked at Alex. Tears were now forming in his eyes as well, but he was more expert at concealing them than I was. "Look at him. He's my boy. He's my baby boy."

"He's *not* your baby boy. He's mine. *You* weren't here for the year I've been raising him. *You* didn't change his diapers at four in the morning. *You* didn't have to deal with all the bad babysitters. *You* had no worries. You were just the big bad football star. Meanwhile, I'm a fucking cliché. I'm a single mother, struggling to keep this household normal. And I'm just fucking it all up. Everything."

He placed his hands on my shoulders and began massaging them gently. "Hey, none of this is your fault. You know that? You're an amazing mother. I already know that much. I can see it in you. You're strong, beautiful, and caring. You're crying because you've given this your all. Alex will know that. He'll understand. Trust me. Remember, I had a deadbeat dad too."

I looked at him in his destructive eyes but quickly looked away. It was all too hard to bear. "I'm sorry. But I don't think we should see each other. It's not good for Alex."

"I want to be in his life, Laura. If I can't have you, at least let me see my son. I'll give him everything I can. I promise. He's our boy."

"Look, can you just leave? I can't even think about any of this now. I have a flight in the morning.

Fuck, I have a flight!" I just remembered I would be going to New York tomorrow. I checked my phone email and saw the ticket and a note from my manager saying: "Safe travels. Make us proud." None of that seemed important now. It all just seemed plastic and fake. What the hell was I doing? What was I *ever* doing?

"Sure. I'll leave. Whatever you want, brown eyed girl." He got up from the couch and closed his fist tightly. "I'll be in Boston tomorrow. We have a hometown game. New York is only a few hours trip. Can I at least see you for dinner or something? We *need* to talk more about this."

"Why Liam? What else do we really need to discuss? You got me pregnant, left me to fend for myself, and now my life is a constant struggle. I'd quit my job and move back to the country if I thought that would help both me and Alex. God, this is all so fucked up. What have I done? Look, why don't you just get back together with that bitch again?"

"Cindy? Jesus Christ. You really don't know me, do you? You think I'm some monster? Some monster who wants to be with some witch? Fuck, Laura. I just want you. That's what I've been trying to tell you this whole damn time!"

"Just. Leave." I said. I was too depressed to think, too confused to even utter more than a few words.

"Fine. But I'm calling you tomorrow before practice. And if you don't answer, I won't be on that field. I'll be on a train to New York City."

I put my hands on my temples and sighed. "Goodbye." I said. That's when he walked out. There was no turning around this time.

Liam

Well, that was the fucking worst night of my life. How could she not tell me I had a son? A son! It was hard to tell whether or not if I was mad or proud. He was a cute little thing, that was for sure. He had her eyes and my nose. He probably had our knack for being a total champion.

Alright, I was pretty damn proud, despite what his mom wanted from me. She claimed she wanted me to get out of her life for good. But I knew that I couldn't just give up. I had to keep trying on this. It was far too important. I was willing to go all of the way too. If she wanted me to quit football for him, I would. I was prepared to do anything to be that kid's father.

I flew back to Massachusetts and immediately started to prepare for the next game. I met with all my trainers, agents, managers, and coaches – all within a day too. I had a lot on my plate and the sadistic thing was, I actually kind of liked it. My phone rang. *Laura!* I thought.

I grabbed it and checked the screen. The name CINDY flashed bright as sin on the screen. *Fuck me.* I mumbled. I hit the green call button and answered it. "What now?" I asked.

"Seriously?" She replied. "You're really going to keep treating me this way? I've called you over 50 times, Liam. 50! You'd think you'd give me a call back by now."

"After the fifth call you should have realized I don't want anything to do with you. Come to think of it, after I told you I didn't is when you should have realized that. Now what the hell do you want?"

She gave a cold cackle into the phone. "I just wanted to talk to you, sweetie. How have you been? I'm in Los Angeles and it is beautiful. Wish you could come to the beach and fuck me in the water like you used to." She said, moaning.

"We never used to do that, Cindy. Come on. Why are you in LA anyway? What business do you have there?" It was weird for her. She never left Dallas.

"I came there for you, sweetie." She laughed. "I wanted to see your big game. I knew you'd make a comeback. You always do."

That took me off guard a bit. "You flew to Los Angeles to see me play? Are you crazy?"

"Shut up, Liam. Your cruel jokes are never funny to me."

"I'm not joking. I'm serious, I want to know. Are you crazy?" I asked her. I didn't have time for this. I needed to call Laura or she might actually believe that I'm a dead beat father.

"No, I am not crazy. I think you might be. How could you fuck that girl?" She asked me. I nearly dropped the phone, smashing it to bits.

"What are you talking about?" I said through my clenched jaw.

"Don't play coy with me, Liam. I saw her watching you up in the box. I saw you point to her on the field." She said.

"You're fucking insane." I wasn't holding back anymore. This time she had gone too far.

"You want to know what I think? I think she's a dumb whore who plays hard to get to keep you around."

"Great. I don't give a shit about what you think. Leave me the fuck alone." I spit angrily into the receiver.

"You'll be sorry." She simply said. "If you ignore me. You'll be sorry."

I turned red and nearly blacked out. Me, sorry? Fuck her. Fuck that audacity. "Don't call me ever again." I said. I hung up the phone and nearly punched the wall in front of me.

I took a few deep breaths, counted to ten, and finally cooled myself off. *Just think of Laura,* I thought to myself. She was the answer to everything.

So I called her. I just hoped I wasn't to her what Cindy was to me. I hoped her hatred was temporary, even if I understood her extreme resentment. I would prove to her that I was the one, and I'd be the best damn father in the world to him.

She answered the phone and whispered, "Hi."

"Did you get them?" I asked her.

"Yeah I got them. Very beautiful. Did your assistant send them over? She must have spent some money to get them shipped by morning." She said sarcastically.

"No." I laughed. "I got them hand picked, just for you. My driver dropped them off at your door early in the morning. Anyway, how was your flight? You made it in okay?"

"Well, thanks I guess. They don't make up for everything that's happened, but it is a sweet gesture. Flight was fine. I'm missing Alex. Where are you right now? Aren't you supposed to be preparing for the game tomorrow morning?" I could hear the sounds of the city blasting into the phone. I wished I was with her, walking through Central Park, eating dinner with Alex and her in Little Italy. Those were the real things that mattered in life. Family and happiness. Not football games and partying. No, suddenly those things didn't seem all that fulfilling anymore.

"I practiced all day today. I'll be fine. I just needed to hear that sweet voice of yours, baby." I said. It was the damn truth too.

"Don't call me baby. I have to go. The producer's here, Call me tomorrow or something. After your game."

"Okay, baby. I'll be seeing you soon." I hung up the phone and made my way to the locker room. Practice was starting and, whether I liked it or not, I had to keep that winning streak going.

Laura

The producer picked the restaurant. A fancy Italian joint in the heart of Brooklyn. It was wonderful. We sat in a clean corner of the outside area and I couldn't help but feel like I was right at home.

"So, you ready for your own show?" He asked me. He was a pudgy bald man with a thick nose. His eyes were round and full, and beads of sweat hung on his forehead like morning dew. He wasn't my cup of tea, but he *was* the producer, so I had to play nice.

I leaned forward and made sure not to break eye contact. "Jacob, I've got my own show now. I imagine this will be something of the same, just with more content. Right?" His eyes left mine as he gazed at my tits. If this wasn't an important business meeting, I would have slapped him for it. "Are you listening to me?" I asked him, getting annoyed by his silence.

"What? Oh yes!" He had regained his sense of self and replied, "Well, honey. It's not *exactly* the same. This is another stepping stone for you. Yes, there will be more content. But with more content comes more responsibility. If you feel good about this, I feel good about this. Got it?"

"Well, I don't feel good about this." I said. He raised his eyebrows. "I feel *great* about this. We're going to fucking kill this, Jacob. Don't even worry. It's all smooth sailing from here on out." I said. He looked relieved. The real truth of the matter was that I had no idea if the show was going to be successful. But you had to dress it up for these guys or they wouldn't take you seriously.

To the men of industry, women like me are just a pair of tits and a nice ass to sit on their faces. Well, I wasn't going to be pigeonholed. This was my new show and I saw it as building my career. By the time I got to Jacob's age, I would fucking run the company and I'd do it better than him or any other man could.

"Good, good." He replied, gulping down his red wine. He grabbed a cigar from his pocket and lit it up. "Is this okay?"

"Do whatever you want. Make yourself comfy. This is your city, after all." I said, smiling.

Moments later, the dinner came out. Fresh lasagna, a side of meatballs, and breaded chicken covered in delicious marinara. It wasn't exactly the wine and dine type of dinner I was used to but I grabbed a small portion of each and dug in. I had a hard week and now it was time for some comfort food.

Inside, something caught my eye. A television was playing loudly and people were yelling at the screen practically every 30 seconds. "What the hell is going on in there?" I asked.

Jacob turned and gasped. "Ah shit! I forgot. Patriots are playing the Giants! I got 4,000 dollars riding on this damn game."

I looked over his shoulder at the TV. I could barely make out the score. 21-14, Patriots lead. On the screen flashed Liam's face. "Oh, God." Jacob mumbled. "That asshole. You know, he's a real prick. Cost me a lot of money."

"That's why you hate the guy? Because he cost you a lot of money?" I asked him, getting slightly defensive.

"Honey, it's not just me. All of New York hates the guy. It's like I said. He's a real prick. You've seen him in interviews, right?"

I nodded, feeling my blood pressure rise. "Yeah. I've seen him." I paused, trying to think of the right words to say.

"And what do you think?" He asked me, very concerned like.

"Ha, well. Let's see. He's sexy, powerful, an incredible player, and yes he's a dick sometimes. But he's one of the best the sport has seen. You can't exactly argue against him."

He looked surprised. A spaghetti noodle hung out his mouth. He burst out laughing. "Sweet-cheeks! You crack me up. You really do, you know that? I think we're going to make a great team, you and I." He laughed.

"Me too, Jacob. Hey, do you think we should have him on the show?" I asked, feeling daring.

"What? Who?" The customers inside roared with cheering as one of the Giants secured a first down.

"Liam Conway. I think he'd make a really good guest. We could have an interview. Maybe follow him on the street. We could call the segment 'A day in the life of Liam Conway.'"

He looked bored. "I'm serious!" I said. "Think about it, Jacob. It would be great. We could bring him out to Brooklyn. We'll have him go to the *most* New York establishments and see how he interacts with business owners and people on the street."

"It would be a disaster." He said with a straight face.

"Exactly! Imagine the ratings bump. People either love or hate Liam. And no matter what side you're on, you'd be watching my show. Right? Don't try and tell me you wouldn't be glued to your damn television, Jacob."

On the television, the subtitles read: "And Conway does it again! He's brought the Patriots to victory! What a throw!"

"Well, I guess I'd tune in for that…" He mumbled. "I still don't know if it's such a good idea. Let's see how the first few episodes do and then we'll talk."

"Aw, c'mon Jacob. Please? For me?" I pouted my lips, leaning over the table. He couldn't resist my charm. He had to oblige.

I actually agreed with Jacob for the most part. It was kind of a stupid idea. But the ratings would be good enough for the networks to be cool with it and since I knew that Liam would come to New York or Los Angeles to talk about Alex regardless, I might as well make it more about business than anything else. I was still pissed as hell at him.

"I don't know, Laura. It's like I said, just wait a minute and see how the show does…" He mumbled.

I grabbed my phone from my purse and started dialing. "I'll tell you what, Jacob. Since you don't think it can be done, let's ring him up and see if he's available. If he isn't, then we'll throw the idea away. But if he is, let's negotiate. If I can bring him down to a good number for you, what's the harm? It's just a guest." I said. He still looked hesitant, but I brushed it off and dialed anyway.

The phone rang against my steady and patient ear. If I was forced to see Liam again, I might as well have some fun with it, right? Finally, after the 5th ring, he answered. "Hey, sorry, I'm in the locker room. What's up? Did you watch the game?" He asked me. It was hard not to laugh, as I felt the wine warming up my face and body.

"Yeah, I kind of watched it. But I have bigger eggs to fry right now. Hey, so real quick, I have a question for you." Jacob was shaking his head and wiping the beads of sweat off his forehead with his napkin. He began motioning for me to hang up. I put my hand out and clasped his, whispering "Stop it."

"Alright, busy girl. What do you need from me? Anything for my babe." He said. What an arrogant prick.

"First of all, I'm not your babe. Second of all, how would you like to be on my new show for half your asking price?" I smiled at Jacob who was now confused to high hell.

Liam coughed loudly. "Half? Sounds like a terrible deal. I'll take it." He said.

"You'll do it? Great!" I yelled. Some of the guest turned to look at me.

"Yeah, of course I'll do it. Does this mean I've earned some points with you? Can I see my son yet?" He asked.

"Don't start with me, Liam." I whispered, cupping my phone. I glanced at Jacob who now looked more bored than anything. "Thanks for doing this. I'll text you my address, can you be here in three days?" I asked.

"Yeah, I think I can work something out. We'll have a couple days together."

"Don't press issue." I laughed and hung up the phone.

I turned and looked at Jacob. "So what's for dessert?"

Liam

Days had passed and the game was becoming easier and easier to play. All I had to do was channel my innermost desires and play as if they were on the line. Right now, Alex and Laura were the two things I would fight for. If I didn't have them, I had nothing. I truly believed that.

"You're crazy, man." Jenkins told me over the phone one day. "She's just pussy. That's it. You don't think I've got kids around some of the cities we played in? Shit, I've got like three. I send the women checks and I get to keep my life intact."

"Great. Sounds like you've got everything under control." I said sarcastically. I shook my head, actually disgusted by the thought of that.

"Brother, it's what we do. We're sports players. We don't live for the family life. We live for the game. That's it. You know, I'm actually starting to worry about you. You're playing good again, but maybe you need a rebound or some shit to get over this girl of yours."

"You're wrong, Jenkins. I'm sorry, but it's not like that for me anymore. I love the game. But this woman comes first. And the baby, that's my flesh and blood, bro. You don't understand. He needs me there. He needs me to take care of him." It was hard to convince him and I understood why. But I wasn't like that anymore. I wasn't a hound dog, trying to fuck every chick in sight. That was the old Liam Conway.

That was the scope of the conversations I had about the situation. The *only* person who really gave a fuck and understood where I was coming from was Coach Stevens. Every time I saw him, he'd ask me for an update. And as things progressed in my life, I played better. I had more determination to succeed and I attributed it all to the two I loved most.

Well, I took a few days off to head to the city. The Big Apple, home of our rivals. I actually liked it out there though. It felt synthetic and real all at the same time. It was a lot different from Dallas, I'll say that much.

My driver dropped me off in the heart of Manhattan, right at Laura's beautiful new home. She answered the door and ushered me in.

She was wearing a button down pink sun dress, and boy did she look hot as fire. I wanted to fall on my hands and knees, and crawl underneath the flowing cotton. I wanted to lap at her like a dog. I wanted to consume her core, until she felt wholly good inside and out. Instead, I kissed her cheek and said, "You look beautiful."

"Shut up." She smiled. "You're trying too hard now and it's not going to work."

"I mean it. You're scorching right now. Like drop dead gorgeous." I put my hand around her waist and felt the warmth of her body. Her face turned flush and she pushed me away lightly.

"Thank you. You look good too." She said. I got it. She didn't want to let up too easy. I still had to earn her trust back. I was cool with that. Still, it was hard not to kiss her, touch her, and pull her in close to me. "Come on. The camera crew is in the other room."

As we walked into the other room, I started to feel hesitant about all of this. "What exactly do you want me to do?" I asked her plainly.

She looked at me and said, "Honestly, nothing crazy. You owe me that interview. I'm just making you come through on your promise. I'm not going to exploit you, don't worry. I have too much respect for you to do that."

I thought back to the day I met her. Me, being the prick I am, saying whatever the fuck I wanted to. I remembered how she hung her head when she realized I wasn't going to say something nice. That was when I knew I wanted her more than anything. There wasn't any logic to it. I just did. I promised her the interview of a lifetime and I was going to give her more than that.

"Liam, meet our producer, Jacob. Over here is the camera crew."

From the moment I saw him, I hated him. He was too close with Laura, always rubbing his greasy hands on her shoulder, telling her what to do. I didn't like guys like him. He was the kind of guy who got picked on in high school, the kind of guy who got a taste of money and used it to prey on beautiful women. He was a disgusting piece of trash.

"Nice to meet ya." I muttered. "So what's the plan?"

Jacob was eyeing me with a smile in his face. I could see the dollar signs flash in his pupils. I hated producers as much as I hated any kind of manager, agent or CEO. They were all suits to me, one in the same.

"We'll start out with an interview. I think we should talk about your family life growing up. People love that kind of stuff. We'll cut the scenes with you enjoying a day in New York City."

"Sounds good, boss." I said.

I sat down in the chair, feeling the burning hot light shine across my face. Laura sat down in front of me, crossing her legs. I wanted to pounce on her, right here. I needed her so fucking badly.

"Liam Conway, I'm extremely excited to have you on the show."

"Thanks, Laura. It's great to be here." I said.

Jacob jumped in and yelled, "Cut, cut, cut! Let's do it over."

"What's the problem?" Laura asked him.

He looked over at me and smiled condescendingly. "Liam. What can I do for you to make you relax? You want a beer? Hey Samantha, get him a beer." He called out to an assistant.

"What are you talking about? I'm fine." I was already this close to socking him.

"Get him a damn beer, Samantha!" He yelled at his assistant again.

"Do not get me a beer, Samantha." I said, clenching my jaw tight.

"Let up, Jacob." Laura warned him.

But he wasn't letting up. He apparently wanted to get his nose broken in by me. "Liam, I apologize. I just want the interview to go well. I have a network to run and what we air needs a certain *umph* to it. It was an okay start, but why don't we get that Liam Conway personality out a bit more." He said.

"I don't know what you're fucking talking about." I said back at him, standing up now.

Jacob clapped his hands together loudly. "Yes! There it is! That attitude. It's you, Liam we need more of that. That's the Liam our audience knows and loves." He was smiling directly at me. I was fuming.

"You don't know me, pal." I said.

"Jacob, relax. I got this. The interview will be good. Can you just go home or something? You're making this kind of difficult." Laura interjected. Her face was red with embarrassment. Now it was personal for me.

"Difficult? Laura, sweetie. What's difficult is pleasing the audience." He walked behind her and placed his hands on her shoulders. His fingers slid over, practically onto the top of her breasts. "How 'bout you leave me to the decision making, honey. I'll steer this in the right direction. You trust me, don't you?"

I didn't even give her a chance to respond. "Don't touch her." I said. It was an easy thing to understand. Apparently for him, it was rocket science.

"What?" He asked me.

"You don't touch a lady unless she asks you to." I repeated.

"Why don't you mind your own business, jerkoff." He said to me. That got me going.

I was on my feet, fists tightened with rage and fury. I swung back my arm as if I were about to throw the winning pass. Then, with the speed of a hundred horses, my knuckles came crashing down on his nose and jaw. *Crack!* I felt his cartilage shatter against my hand. Of course that little slimy man brought out the anger in me. It's what he wanted from me right? Well, he got it. He got it good.

"Liam!" Laura yelled, jumping toward Jacob. "Oh my God. Jacob, I am so sorry. I had no idea he would do this!" She looked at me as if I were the devil.

"Ah shit." I muttered. "Look, I was just trying to protect the lady, okay? You understand right?" I helped him up. Blood was crusted on his jacket.

"My nose! I'll sue you, asshole! I'll sue the both of you! You'll never get any work in this town. That much I can promise you both! Fuck!" He yelled, stomping around the room like a child.

"I'll pay for the hospital bill and some. Just don't fucking touch people like that. They're not your objects, brother." I was justified. I knew I was. The guy was a creep. I just did what others were too scared to do. He wouldn't sue me. They never did. I turned to Laura and said, "I'm really sorry."

"Just. Leave." She said with tears in her eyes. Her face was harsh, but she looked more heartbroken than angry. *Fuck, just when I was going to make it up to her,* I thought to myself.

Laura

The next day was spent in the hospital with Jacob. Liam vowed to make everything right. He *needed* to set things straight. Or so he said. Here were the facts: the father of my child had punched my producer and my show was hanging by a thread. I was a wreck. Not that I wasn't before.

I begged and I begged until finally Jacob conceded. He would let the show continue, as long as I never brought Liam onto the show ever again. The episode, however, would have to wait. Production would be halted. I would have to go back to Los Angeles until his nose and jaw had healed. *God dammit...*

So I flew back to LA, despite it all. Liam, being the man he is, decided to come with. We flew in a jet that belonged to the team. Of course, I was bit too angry to enjoy the ride. I sat staring out the window, at the never-ending shapes of the world below.

"I'm really fucking sorry. I know I've got a pretty bad temper." He said when we got back to my place. I simply looked away from him. It wasn't even that I was mad at him for punching Jacob. The truth was Jacob was a creep and he deserved much more than that. It was that he lived a life where he felt entitled to do whatever it is he wanted to do. All celebrities were like this.

"I just don't know if I can trust you anymore." It was as if the words were just floating out of my mouth. It was the truth and I couldn't help how I felt.

"What can I do to make you trust me again? Please Laura. I'll do anything. I want to be with you. I want to raise Alex with you. At least let me try." He pleaded. But they were just words. Things people say. They didn't mean anything. Only actions held real weight.

"Nothing. Just be a normal person, okay? For once in your life, be what you say you'll be." I said, pushing him close to the door.

"So you're just going to kick me out then? Fine. I'll leave." He said, arrogantly shaking his head at me.

"Good!" I screamed back, slamming the door. I fell onto the hard wood floor, back against the shut door. Alex simply stared at me.

"I'm sorry kiddo." I said. "Mommy's just tired."

He crawled his cute butt toward me as I held my arms out for him. He was so damn precious, his smile could turn a shit day into something really special. But when he finally got to me, he grabbed at the bottom of the front door and actually spoke his first words: "Dadda?" He pointed toward the front yard. "Dadda go?" He asked me.

His first words. I felt the night sky envelop me. What could a lady do if there was no one to trust?

Liam

I slammed the door behind me, shaking with confusion and anger. I had fucked up again. Only this time it was different. This time I had made the only woman I cared for hate me. Correction: she didn't *hate* me. She just didn't trust me anymore. There was a huge difference when it came to those words. And losing trust was much, much worse.

I walked along the main boulevard, hands in my pocket, head arched toward the night sky. The sharp moonlight shined down on me, bathing me in its mysterious glory. "What can I do?" I asked the night sky. "How can I fix this?" Images of my child flashed through my mind. His smile, his face, the way he crawled toward me. He was so damn peaceful when he was next to me. It's like he knew.

Even if he didn't, I had to figure things out. I wasn't a guy that just gave up when the going got tough. I kept walking, thinking to myself. I walked past a television store. I stopped to see the headlines. On the stack of TV's was my face. "Rage of Fury" flashed on the screen. Then the words "Crazy Patriot."

The screen panned to ESPN's correspondent Chelsea Haywahl. *"Hello and welcome everybody. Tonight we have an odd story for you. You may know Liam Conway as the star quarterback of both the Patriots and the Cowboys. Well, now it seems he's gotten into a little bit of trouble. Chris Hughes is in New York City with the story."* The camera then panned to Chris Hughes in front of the Chrysler Building. It looked like a fake backdrop but I wasn't too sure.

"Trouble in Paradise is the headline for today. I'll tell you why. Liam Conway, super-quarterback for the Patriots has assaulted someone yesterday and it turns out it's none other than the producer for our own network."

I stopped watching. It wasn't worth my time. In my pocket my phone vibrated. My PR agents were going crazy. One of the texts read "Call me back

ASAP. The Press is having a field day with you. We need to issue a calculated response." I sighed and shook my head. I could never catch a damn break.

I wasn't a psychopath. I wasn't a murderer or sadist, nor was I some power-hungry asshole. I was just a ball player. That's it. A ball player with a mild problem with his temper and agitation. Was that really all that unusual?

No one knew me. No one. Not even Laura. I wanted her to figure me out, but I was like a locked box wrapped a million times over. I was hard to grasp.

When my father left us, it ruined me. I was just six years old. A child. He left my mom, sure. Men and women do that all the time to each other and it's heart breaking. But there was one thing I couldn't ever get over. I caught him sneaking out one night. He had a backpack and a suitcase, a few loose items, and a look on his face that said "I'm out of here."

I said, "Dad? Where you going?"

He leaned over to me and whispered, "Go back to bed. I'm going on a little trip. I'll be back before you know it."

Something seemed fishy, however. I asked him, "Can you take me with you? I want to go on a trip too." Anything to be around pops. Anything.

"No." He whispered. "Mommy wouldn't like that. You have to be a good boy because good boys get what they want. Are you going to be good for me?" He whispered. But I knew what that meant. Being a good boy meant keeping your mouth shut. Being a good boy meant acquiescing to bad people making bad decisions. But I was too young to fight back. I was too young to know how to scream for my mom to keep him there. Besides, it wasn't up to her anyway. He would have beat both of us if I spoke up. I had to let him go. I had to ...

* * *

I turned away from the TV's and I grabbed my phone and threw it into the busy road. It smashed into a million pieces underneath a truck's tire. I wasn't crazy, dammit. I just loved someone.

I stopped dead in my tracks. That's right. I *loved* her. And I wasn't about to stop loving her anytime soon. I kept walking, aimless and confused, until I walked by an odd flower store. I stopped. It was 9 PM but the store was open for a few more minutes. I walked inside.

"Good evening." A kind woman said to me.

"I need flowers. Lots of flowers." I found myself saying.

"Well you came to the right place. How many do you need?" The woman asked me, cutting off the stems from a pair of roses.

"Enough to fill a yard." I said. "Enough to say I'm sorry and I love you more than anything in this bullshit world. Enough to say…" My words fell short as the woman smiled a familiar smile.

"I think I can help you." She said. "Come."

She opened a back door and inside was a room full of fresh cut floral arrangements. "I'll take them all." I said. "In fact, I'll take the whole damn store."

Laura

It was supposed to be an easy life. That's what was always promised to me. Instead, it was all heartache and pain. The thing was, I couldn't even talk to Katherine about it anymore. Every time I brought it up, she would respond in a callous way. It was as if my troubles meant nothing to her.

I had no one to rely on anymore, besides my family. Not my friends, definitely not my producers or agents, and not the father of my child. My parents were basically clueless when it came to the kind of life I led. It would have been easy to give up right then and there. But I didn't.

When I woke up the next morning it was still dark outside. The sound of violins rang out against the morning air. Wait, *violins*? *Must be a part of my dream*, I thought to myself. But the sound continued. I slowly climbed out of bed, aching and still barely awake, and opened the door. I squinted against the full moonlight.

The most bizarre thing happened to me. Outside my home was a full orchestra, all dressed up as if they were going to the play a big concerto. "What the hell?" I whispered. I walked out onto the front steps of my lawn and sat down.

It was beautiful. All around the players were large wreaths, roses, tulips, and just about any other flower you could imagine. In the center were giant letters. I tried to read them but they were too big from below. I ran into the backyard and climbed on my roof. It would be a nicer view from up there anyway.

I struggled to push my feet onto the rooftop. When I finally secured a foothold, I slipped and fell backward. "No!" I screamed, sure as hell I was falling to my death. That's when I felt a warm pair of hands grab mine. I looked up, hanging off the roof. It was Liam.

"Let me help you." He said, pulling me up onto the roof with him. When I was finally safe, I looked at him angrily. "Just let me explain." He said, walking to the front edge of the house. "Look."

We both sat down, our feet dangling over the edge. The orchestra was playing the delicate strings as the city lights twinkled in the distance. It was a picturesque sight to see.

"You know, I've never been up here." I admitted. "The whole city is visible up here. It's incredible."

"Sometimes they best things in life are right in front of your eyes. You just have to look at it in a different way to see them." Liam said.

I looked down at the letters built by petals and stems. "I love you." It said. A simple, yet special message. My stomach sank and my heart began to flutter. "Oh, Liam…" I whispered.

"To the ends of the earth and back." He said, wrapping his arms around me. The cold breeze of the morning-night circled around our bodies. "I was born to win. But it wasn't the game that I was supposed to win. I was born so I could win your love. Now, I may have fucked it all up. I know I've got some problems.

But that doesn't mean you shouldn't love me. I'll prove to you that I'm the one. I *love* you." He stopped speaking and looked at me, waiting for a response.

I laid my head against his shoulder and gave a sigh of odd relief. "This is the most special thing anyone has ever done for me." I said.

"There's more where that came from. Every day of our life together will be a gift." He whispered, his lips against the top of my head. I felt so close to him, despite what had happened. And yet, it was like there was a small wall built in between us.

"But how can I trust you?" I asked him. "How will I know you won't do something stupid like that again?"

"This is a new era for me. I'm not going to be the same man I was." He said. And then he admitted something to me. Something I never knew about before. "When I was a young boy, probably around four or five. Maybe even six. My father was a strict man. He didn't like it when things weren't going smooth as ice around the house. If, say, a cup was left on the counter for more than a day, he'd flip on you.

He'd push the cup off the counter, smash it into a million pieces and slap your face. 'You gonn' know what being bad is all about.' He would say. Well, me and my mom tried to do better, but it was like walking on eggshells around him. One small thing would set him off. Then, right before he left us, he started to act crazy. Like, really crazy. The slaps turned into full on punches. I'd find my mom bleeding on the bathroom floor, unable to scream for help. The whole house was full of fear and paranoia. Anger and utter sadness." He took a deep breath, even though I knew those tears were about to start coming. He tried to hold them back, his lip trembling as he spoke.

"Liam. My God... That's horrible." I said to him. I didn't know what else to say. He kept speaking.

"And it got to the point where my mom had to go to the hospital one time. He broke her nose. Shattered her septum. Bruised her ribs. He would..." He choked up during this part and shook his head, as if he was trying to shake the memory for good. "He would do worse to her. Things I don't even want to talk about, you know? I was just a child and she was just a mother trying to provide for her child. But him? He was the devil. I'm sure of it. I know you can't trust me, Laura. And I know I need to defeat those memories inside of me. I need to get rid of that anger and pain to fix my reactions to certain people. But know that I would be the best God damn father to Alex. I would give him more than I would give myself. And I would *never,* ever leave you two. Not in a million years." He stopped talking and breathed calmly, wiping away the tears from his eyes.

"I misjudged you." I said. "From the very start, I thought of you as someone you aren't. I thought you were an asshole, a jock that couldn't control himself. Now I'm thinking, maybe I should see where you've grown and where you're struggling. Maybe…" I turned to him. "Maybe, I should be there for you like you'd be there for me."

He smiled and ran his hands through my hair, caressing the back of my head. He kissed my soft cheek. "I don't deserve anything." He said. "But I *need* you. It's crazy how much I love you."

"Everyone deserves a second chance, right? I'll try my best to forgive you." I said. "Just promise me you'll be trustworthy from now on. I can't be with someone who's going to destroy my career or spit in my cameraman's face." I laughed slightly, not because it was all that funny. However, up against the moonlight, small sliver of sunlight, and music playing from the violins and cellos, it didn't seem all that big. I don't know. It was like the feeling of forgiveness had rushed inside my heart.

He nodded and massaged the knots from my neck. "I know I wouldn't want that kind of thing from you either. Cindy would do rash things all of the time. She would yell in cameras, pull up her shirt in front of people, and get far too fucked up. I hated that about her, so why should I do that to you? I'm just sorry. For everything." He whispered.

"I forgive you." I whispered, running my hands across his warm chest. I kissed his stomach and closed my eyes. Things would be better from here on out. They had to be.

"Liam?" I whispered.

"Yes, my brown eyed girl?"

"I love you too."

It wasn't too long before we fell asleep together, our backs against the tiles of the roof. The morning sunlight eventually found its way over the valleys and mountains at the edges of the world. All was good in my world. No. All was perfect.

Liam

"Come on. There you go! Wow, you're so big and strong!" Alex was running toward me, arms wide open, roaring like a dinosaur.

"Oh my God!" Laura yelled. He's never ran this far before!

"You can do it buddy!" I said. He fell over, but immediately picked himself back off the ground. He looked at me and dove into my arms, giggling loudly. "You did it! I can't believe you made it this far!"

"Dadda! I did eat." He said, jumbling his words.

"I cannot believe he's talking this much. It doesn't make sense. He never said a word around me." She smiled. Around us were kids playing on the swing sets, mothers and fathers reading on the benches or looking at their phones. Most of the parents weren't even paying attention to their kids.

"It was just time, probably." I reasoned. "He's getting older everyday."

She sighed. "I know. Time goes by so fast. It seems like it was just yesterday when we first met."

"Momma! Love!" Alex squealed. "Love Momma!"

I practically saw her heart shatter into a million pieces. Shatter with love, of course.

With the biggest smile I've ever seen on her face, she kissed his belly and picked him up into her eyes. "You want to swing? You want mommy to push you?"

He nodded his head and clapped his hands in apparent approval. "Okay!" She said, setting him into the seat of the kids swing. She pushed him ever-so-lightly and watched as he had the fucking time of his life. It was incredible to see. Imagine your son, the one you somehow created is now blasting off into space just from one small push on a swing.

I stood in front of him, holding a plush football, smaller than his head. "Alex! Go long!" I yelled, throwing it in his direction. It landed in the swing of his seat. He cheered as if he had just scored a touchdown of his own.

After a few minutes, we had all begun to get tired. In the distance, the sun was beginning its second half of rotation for the day. In just a few hours, the sun would set, and all the little babies of the world would be put to sleep. I turned to Laura and kissed her beautiful marble skin.

"I never thought Alex would have anyone in his life. Like, I got pregnant and I just thought, 'this could be easy. I can do this by myself.' Boy was I naïve." She said, laying down on the grass with me and our child.

"You could have done it. It just takes some getting used to." I said, admiring her strength. She had done so much already.

"I guess you're right. It's not the same though. A boy needs his daddy. He needs a male figure like that in his life. It was as if the moment Alex saw you he changed. He spoke his first words. He was running. You energize him, Liam. You give him such strength."

"He's easy to love." I said. Anything that comes from you must be an angel. I'm really not looking forward to going back to Massachusetts." I said, remembering I had some big games to play. They were the playoff games and I needed to play my best if my team wanted to get anywhere near the Super Bowl.

"It won't be all that bad." She reasoned. "I'll be in New York. It's not far. And I'll come to all the games in the region, I promise. Plus, you'll have fun being with the boys again."

I nearly burst out laughing. "Fun? The whole NFL hates me right now. The Patriots are probably wondering what the hell they've gotten into. I'm not exactly a picture perfect sports player in my agents' eyes." I said.

"Hey, just look at this way. You're not as bad as OJ Simpson."

"Fuck, I sure hope not." We picked ourselves up and headed for the car.

In just a few days I would be back "home." I would jump back into training, and practice, all the while trying to make a good name for myself. I knew it would be rough at first. I knew my mates would shun me. But when was I ever *not* shunned? That was kind of my thing. As for right now, I had a son to raise. And that wasn't so bad either.

Laura

"Does Liam Conway have what it takes? He's had a few good games out there lately, but can he take it home every single night? That's the question we're all asking ourselves this morning as the New England Patriots take on the Denver Broncos!" I flipped on the pre-game show and sat down with Alex to watch. Footage of Liam on the field was flashing on the screen.

"I'm so glad you're in town!" I yelled at the kitchen. Katherine was in the city for just two days and we were lucky enough to have her as a guest.

"Yeah? Well, expect a lot more of me. I have totally won the lottery at work." She smiled, spooning at her banana split.

I grabbed her cherry and quickly ate it, smiling. I said, "I'm *so* happy you got that promotion. You have no idea! California Rep for Dior is a huge deal!"

"It's a lot of travel time, but it means I get to leave Dallas every month. Can't beat that." She said.

"Wait, wait! He's on." I cried out.

The screen cut to an interview from days before, *"I know in my heart that we'll be the next Super Bowl champions. It's just a matter of time at this point."*

"How do you know, Liam?" The reporter asked him.

He shrugged and smiled, *"Because I'm the best."*

"There's that cocky attitude we know and love. Although, let's just hope he can keep his temper in control at this morning's game."

"Oh, bullshit!" I yelled at the commentators, forgetting I was still holding Alex. "Don't ever say those words." I whispered, kissing his head.

Katherine was staring at me, complete with this odd looking smile on her face. After a full minute of this, I turned to her and threw my hands up. "What? Why are you staring at me like that?"

"You are in *love*!" She screamed. Alex clapped his hands loudly and giggled.

"I am not." I blushed.

She stopped me. "Girl. I know what love looks like and it's in your eyes. Don't try to play games." She leaned forward excitedly and clasped her hands together. "So, does he know?"

I covered my face and blew out loudly. "Ugh."

"Come on! You have to tell me! I'm your best friend and you haven't called me in weeks. I thought you may have died out here. I expected to come here and find a corpse in the bedroom!" She joked.

"Stop it." I pressed my face into my shirt and breathed in deeply. "He knows. Alex knows. We all know. We're one big happy family."

"Seriously? Oh my God!" She cackled.

"Settle down. It's not a big deal. We're, uh, working things out. We'll see where it goes from there." I said.

She took a big bite of ice cream and, moaning with pleasure, said, "You better be careful. Did you hear how he mangled some producer? I heard he had to get complete reconstructive surgery. I know sports players are kind of crazy, but do you really think Alex needs that kind of aggression around the house?" Alex, more perceptive than we probably even know, started to cry.

"Come on, Alex." I said. I picked him up into my arms and walked toward his room.

"Oh, stop! I didn't mean anything by it. Seriously. I'm sorry." She called out to me, biting her nails.

"Daddy!" Alex yelled, pointing to the screen.

"I know, I know. But you have to go to bed, my sweet." I whispered.

I set him down in his crib and kissed Alex's face. "You're getting heavy, aren't you? Pretty soon, we'll have to get you a big boy's bed." I reached in to his crib and grabbed his favorite toy, the plush football his father had given him. I began to tear up uncontrollably. Pretty soon he would be old enough to be an adult. Time had already seemed to go a million miles per hour these days.

I walked back into the living room and sat down next to Katherine. "I've already thought a lot about it." I said. "I'm willing to give him a second chance. You should see him with Alex. He's an incredible father to him."

"Alright." She said.

We sat and watched the game for what seemed like hours. The weird thing was, I actually kinda liked it! What used to be a boring game of first downs, end zone passes, and massive ab muscles, now gave me a huge rush of adrenaline and excitement.

The television burst with the noise of cheering. *"Liam Conway himself just ran the ball into the end zone! He is definitely the coach's favorite right now and for good reason. If they win this game, they will be entering the Super Bowl Championships."*

Another commentator replied, *"That's what happens when you try and sack Liam Conway. It just can't be done. The game as it currently stands is 28-3, Patriots' favor. I am loving every second of this, Chris!*

"He's got this." I whispered to myself. Katherine looked over at me and laughed. "He's going to take them to the Super Bowl!" I yelled, suddenly getting very into the game.

On the field, Liam was looking left and right, calling out numbers and observing the defense. When he finally felt comfortable, the command came. *"Hike!"* The ball came spiraling back at him. A lineman had broken through the offensive guards, and Liam turned and ducked to get out of the way. Looking aimlessly, he finally found Charlie ten yards in the distance. He lobbed the ball in his direction and was immediately tackled. The ball didn't come close to Charlie.

"No!" I yelled, jumping onto my feet. "Come on! That's a foul or something!" I turned to Katherine, "Right?"

She shrugged, "Hell if I know. But it's really entertaining watching you freak out over something you barely understand."

"Wait! One second…" I said, getting her to quiet down. On TV, Liam was arguing with the player that had tackled him. He threw up his hands in frustration and ripped his helmet off. The other player shoved Liam, nearly knocking him down.

"Please don't do it, Liam." I pleaded at the screen. "Don't let me down…" Katherine was eyeing me carefully.

Players from both teams came running onto the field to make sure a fight didn't happen. Liam threw his helmet onto the ground and wound his arm back quickly. "No!" I screamed. His fist came barreling through the air, cutting into his jaw. The man fell backward onto the turf, clearly unconscious.

"He's done." I mumbled. "He's so done."

"It was just on the field. It's not that big a deal, Laura. These things happen all the time. What do you expect?" She asked me. But it was too soon after what had happened with my producer. He made a promise to me. He broke that promise only days after.

The rest of the team had now broke out into a full out brawl. Charlie, Jimmy, and the rest of the guys were roughing each other up pretty good. Liam was being held down by two officers, squirming for his life to break free.

Finally, a whole squadron of security and police had made their way onto the field to stop this debauchery and violence.

The announcer was exhilarated by this fight. It was everything he had been waiting for and more. "*I have never, ever seen anything like this in my life! Both teams are now battling it out on the field, Chris! It is complete mayhem out there. I said it earlier, hot head Liam Conway's main mission is to destroy the game. That goes for the players too!*"

I held my hands above my head, screaming and shaking my fist. "No! No! No!" I cried. "Asshole!"

"*His career, Chris, is on the line right now, and this is not a good light to see him in. I'm sure those sponsors aren't very happy.*"

"Oh, just turn it off. I can't watch anymore of this." I said, turning away from the TV.

Katherine reached for the controller and said, "Well, I'm sure he has a reason for doing what he did out there. The guy *did* shove him."

On the TV they continued, *"Sources are saying that his recent outbursts might be due to the fact that he's been seeing Cindy Rolkins again. Not a good sign, guys. These are, I should say, just rumors and tabloids could be wrong. However, he…"*

Katherine cut the power.

I could barely hold back my fury. "He's been seeing Cindy again? What the fuck?" I hesitated to speak but then got a sudden burst of energy. "You know what? You're probably right. I'm sure he has plenty of reasons why he's been acting this way. The main one being that he's cheating on me!"

"I better go." Katherine sighed. "I'm sorry all this is happening to you, Laura. I really am. You *have* to ditch that loser. If you don't, don't say I didn't warn you. Since when were you into sports players anyway?"

"Katherine, he's the father of my child." I raised my eyebrows at her. You'd think by now she would have gotten the picture. "Anyways, you're probably right. I need to be alone for now. I need to think about everything."

"Alright, dear. Just promise me one thing. Do what will be best for you and your baby, not anyone else. Liam is an adult. He can start to act like one."

Liam

"Fuck it! Fuck it all!" I screamed, punching a dent into the floor below me. "It's all a big fucking sham." Sweat rolled down my eyes, dripping onto my shoes. We had won the game, apparently. Only, they had won it without my help. I was pulled from the game.

Coach Stevens was circling in front of me, weighing his options. The rest of the coaches and my PR agent sat in front of me, arms crossed against their brand new suits.

Stevens said, "What do you want from us, Liam? Do you want us to sit by and do nothing while you cause a mess of a riot on the field? Our job is on the line. Hell, *your* job is on the line."

"They gonna suspend me?" I asked, staring dead into his eyes.

My PR agent stepped in. "The press is already losing their minds over this, Liam. It's worse than suspension. Your sponsors are threatening to pull out. You're quickly becoming a name no one wants to associate with. It's time for you to shape up." He said. Images of my father flashed in my brain. I felt dizzy. Confused. None of this was my fault. If only they knew what the guy had said to me.

He continued speaking. "Is it true you're seeing Cindy again?" He asked.

I nearly fell back in my seat. "What the hell kind of a question is that?"

"She's a toxic person, Liam. She'll get you into trouble. Remember what happened last time when she tried to sue you? The media massacred you."

"She's not just a toxic person. She's a piece of trash on the side of road, a complete mess of a life. I wouldn't see her if you paid me too." I spit out. I suddenly felt very sick to my stomach.

"That's not what she's telling the Enforcer." He said. The Enforcer was everybody's favorite tabloid magazine. They were notorious for over-exaggerating and never fact checking their sources.

"And you believe her? God, what kind of people are you? Quit reading that trash and focus on the game." I said. But I knew I was screwed. At the very least they would suspend me and Laura would break up with me. I tried. I really tried.

He continued, "It's not my job to focus on the game, son. It's my job to focus on what people are saying about you. Now, a hell of a lot of people probably know it's not true. All I'm trying to communicate is that there's a lot of other people who don't. So what we need to do is get a statement circulating in the press. If you're really telling the truth, and for your sake I hope for you are, then we need to denounce her right away."

"What else did she say?" I asked him with a straight face.

The man hesitated and choked on his spit. "She said…" He looked around the room at our coaches. They were currently holding their breath and shaking their heads. "Well, Liam. She's making claims you propositioned her. Multiple times."

"That's a fucking lie!" I screamed. "I would never fuck that troll ever again, you hear me? Never again!"

The coach sighed and waved at me to shut up. "Settle down. I don't need to hear about it anymore. We just need you to take care of everything. Sound good to you."

"Sounds like a plan." I said.

"Alright, everyone. I think you've heard all you need to hear. Now, I'm going to ask you all to leave. I need some time alone with my star player." Stevens said, staring out the window now.

The men around us grumbled and filed outside. As he shut the door, my PR agent leaned inside and said, "Call me right after you get out of here. We'll need a statement. Better yet, let's do a press conference this week too."

"Yeah, sure." I mumbled. "I'll call ya."

The coach closed the door and locked it. He gave a big sigh of stress. Then he did something weird. He actually burst out laughing. "What the

Hell? Is this funny to you?" I asked, confused how any of this was funny to him.

"I *love* your energy, Conway. You're finally playing like you want to win!" He laughed. "Look, let's get down to the truth of the situation here. They're going to suspend you, Liam."

"Fuck." I nearly quit right then and there. In my 20 some years playing ball, I had never missed a game. Never. Now they were talking about a suspension. "How long?"

"One game." He said. "Hey, don't give me that look. You're lucky I had kind words to say about you. The higher-ups wanted you out longer. They said you're a liability for the networks. One game and you'll be back on that field, leading the team to victory."

"Oh yeah? So I guess the game is all about the ratings, huh? Well, that's good news." I said with heavy sarcasm.

"Take a look outside for a second, Liam." He motioned for me to come stand next to him, near the window of the office. "You see that sign? How about that sign there? See that one next to it too? Those three signs supply our team with 2 million dollars. Now, that may not be that much to you. But it pays your bills." He stopped and thought to himself for a second.

"It just feels so plastic. That is all I'm trying to say." I mumbled.

"You knew what you were getting into. No doubt about that. Remember when we recruited you? You must have played over 1000 games. You were the clear front-runner choice. Most kids would have killed to be where you were. When we recruited you, we gave you everything. Drugs, booze, all the girls you could have wanted. We even gave you new cars, a home. We gave you the world. Now you're saying it feels too plastic for you? Liam, come on. This is the big league. You know exactly what they want from you. They chew you up and spit you out. Pretty soon, they make you coach and tell you 'Make this kid better than you were or you're through.' It's rough, but it's what we signed up to do."

"The guy said he knew my new girl. Said he'd been watching her on the streets. Said he heard she was the wettest girl in town. He couldn't wait to have a go with her, that I was less than a man. I can't remember the exact words. But that's more or less what he said to me. And, trust me, he wasn't talking about Cindy." I said. "What do you expect me to do? I had to defend her. No one talks about the woman I love like that. No one."

I stared at the ugly carpet below my feet. It was the carpet stupid rich men placed their desks over and dirtied their shoes on. I doubt these guys even watched the games. No, they probably wake up early, get their memos and drink their coffee, and tell the next person in line what to do. Shit, the players should be running this shit. Instead, we're just a bunch of slaves.

"You're right, coach." I suddenly said. "And you've been good to me. Great, actually. You're my mentor and I'm proud to say that you're my friend too. I know you've always had my back. Times are just hard right now. You know I've got a kid? Found that out about a week ago."

"A kid? With that woman? What're you going to do?" He asked me, now sitting down at the desk.

"The only thing I can do. Raise that child and be the best damn father anyone's ever seen." I said.

Laura

The time had come for Alex and I to stay in New York. I had packed all I needed to pack for the week and took off for the city. My plan was to turn off my phone and dive into the work for my show, but that of course, was impossible to try and pull off.

The morning I got in, I walked to Central Park with Alex, and sat down to enjoy the day. That's when *he* called me. "Liam, stop it." I said. "I don't want to talk to you about this."

He shouted over me. "You don't understand what happened. I've seen the tapes of what happened and it looks worse than it was. This kind of thing happens all the time in football. It's par for the course."

"Which is exactly why I want this to end! I don't like the football life. I don't like the NFL, the stupid Patriots, and I sure as hell don't like the violence they've embedded into you! It's not normal to get in fistfights all the time. I don't want Alex growing up around that kind of lifestyle." I wanted to throw the phone in a nearby pond. This was my one free day with Alex and I wanted it to be good. Instead, I was too busy arguing with his father over something that was *so* over.

"Then I'll quit." He said in defiance. "I'll fucking quit. Would that make you happy?"

"Look, Liam. I don't care what excuse you have for me this time. Nothing is going to change my mind. It's obvious you can't control yourself out there. How will you be able to control yourself here at home when the going gets tough? You're ruining your image and you've made me lose all the trust in the world for you." I said, too angry to cry. "God dammit, Liam. I heard you got suspended too."

"You don't understand, baby. I was suspended for one game. That's it! I—"

"I do understand. I understand a hell of a lot more than you do. For example, I understand that this is over. I understand that *you* and *me* are not connected. We had one silly night. One random, stupid night, and you became obsessed with the idea of being with me. But you don't want to be with me. You want to fight with your *little* friends. You wouldn't be a good father if you tried." It was a harsh sentence to give. The problem was, he wasn't all that bad. I knew that deep down. But this thing we had had gotten too messy. I didn't know how to reconcile it. And this hidden violence that was within him was something I wanted no part in.

We had met. We got lost in our passions. And a life was born from ignorance and too much hopefulness. That was our story.

"I love you." He whispered. I couldn't tell, but from the sound of it, he had given up as much as I had. I gave us what we both needed: I hung up the phone.

I turned to my baby, sweet and innocent. But with every giggle and every smile, I saw him. His nose, the dimples in his cheeks, the color of his hair. It was all Liam.

In the distance were the rides. I remembered as a little girl being taken to the city once. It was the one trip out of the farmland, the one great escape. I remembered my dad holding my up against the wind, and I was screaming as we circled round and round. A million lights spun around us. The tallest buildings in the world towered above. "Someday," He said, "this will all be yours."

"Alex, want to ride the carousel?" I asked him.

"Daddy! Daddy?" He was asking for his father. It was times like these that made it hard for me. Life had a way of fucking things up for everyone. Why did I ever introduce both of them?

"Daddy's not coming. He has a *big* game coming up." I whispered with a huge fake smile on my face. He had begun to cry.

I picked him up and he wrapped his little arms around my neck. Again, I felt Liam. "I'm sorry for everything." I found myself saying to Alex, walking toward the rides. "I know it's been hard for you."

Alex, still crying, was saying nothing. Obviously, he could barely understand the words I was trying to convey. I just had no one to talk to right now. I just wanted to make things right with my baby boy.

"But it's been hard for me too. Your father is… Well, he's different. He's a rough guy. A handsome guy. But his job is scary."

"Scawry?" Alex asked me. I laughed a little. He was learning too fast.

"Yes, scary. He's not a bad guy. He has a good heart. He's just unpredictable. Mommy needs someone who can give his all to you, not someone who's going to give their all to a silly game." I said. We finally got to the carousal. The same one I had rode with my dad a lifetime ago.

"I just wanted to apologize to you now, Alex. Someday you'll be a big, strong man. You'll find a woman you want to take care of and love. When you do, give her 100 percent. Give her your all. Because if you don't, she'll be gone forever." The people all around us looked at me like I was crazy. Maybe I was. All of the stress of this fucked up situation had gotten to my head a bit.

"Two riders for the carousel please." I said to the booth man. I dumped the money into his hand and he handed us the tickets.

I walked up to the wooden booth designed with horses, frogs, and other animals, and set Alex down on my lap. He stared above at the lights and old-style paintings. "It's just you and me now, kid." I kissed his head as the floor beneath us started to spin us into orbit. We were freely spinning, yet connected to all those around us. As hard as it was to see outside our booth, the world was there. It was just dormant. It was waiting for us to slow down.

What I needed, however, was a night out on the town.

Liam

Suspensions aren't for guys like me. They knew just how much they needed me. Which is why I only got one game I had to sit out. Well, one full game turned into one half a game. That is, after all the negotiations went down. Turns out, the fight actually boosted my career. My worth went up like a firework on the Fourth of July. My internet searches skyrocketed. People apparently liked watching me dick around on the field.

But I was still being rejected by the one I loved. I didn't understand – I was trying my hardest. If she knew what that guy had said to me out there, she might've understood. I had nothing else now. It was back to the basics.

I poured myself into training. Whether it was practicing my throws, my weight training, or studying my plays, I devoted my whole and entire life to it. I did this at all hours of the day. I became a fucking monk. It was football or nothing. But I promised myself that when I won this thing and brought my team to the top, I would get Laura back. I'd get her and my baby boy back.

The thing got me the most was that I was actually a good father. I was at least a million times better than my own. Yeah, I made mistakes. But they were the cost of the game. Sometimes you just got into scuffles. It was a hell of a lot better than getting a concussion. Yet, that kind of a thing was swept under the table. Tabloid magazines could give two shits about long term brain injuries. Sex and violence. That's what makes the big bucks.

I was getting bored of all that now, ever since I met Laura. Ever since I met my son. But it was all I had for now.

Even the players were lined against me. They were getting cocky, even when their playing was getting worse. Some fuck-toy on the second-string team even said, "Hey Conway. Now that you're on the outs, mind if I try out some of those signature plays?"

I threw the ball into his shaking hands. "I'd love to see you try, boy." I laughed. Then I got real close to him and muttered, "I know you'll say anything for a reaction, but I'd hold your tongue if I were you."

He kept on smiling, although I know deep down he was shaking in his underwear. "What'll you do? Hit me?" He asked.

"Oh, that's what you're scared of? Me hitting you? No I won't hit you, boy. I'll do much worse. I'll make sure you never play ball again. 'Cause when I win and get this team the Super Bowl Championship trophy like I did with the Cowboys, people will be kissing at my feet. And guess what, partner? When that time comes, I'll be remembering that ugly face of yours."

It was a useless threat, but I had to stand my ground one way or another. My team hated me now. That much I knew. But I wasn't going to forfeit my crown that easily. Besides, I was still the best player on the team.

The entire practice was littered with smart-ass comments and attempts at getting the coaches to side against me. They didn't realize they already were. The narrative was: it's just not safe to put him in yet.

* * *

The night before the game, I went out. It didn't matter anyway, I was sitting out tomorrow regardless. I walked down the strip, searching for the right place to loose myself in booze and sorrow-filled stories. When I finally found a dive bar suitable enough for me to sink into, I did just that.

"I'll take a shot of bourbon." I muttered at the middle-aged bartender. He has a towel slung over his right shoulder, a tucked in black t-shirt, and the hardened look of a criminal.

He turned to me and said, "Ran out of bourbon an hour ago. How 'bout some whisky?"

I gave him a nod of approval, as if to say, "Sure thing, brother. Whatever will get me fucked up fastest."

He poured me a shot and I quickly swallowed it down. "Another." I said, slamming the glass down on the table.

"Alright. You're the boss." He poured another shot. Again, I dropped it back.

"Another." I said, straight faced. I was tired. Not physically or anything, but I was tired of all that bullshit going on around me at all times. Sick of the game, sick of the industry, and sick of the people. The booze was a bandaid of sorts. Only, I knew it wouldn't help anything. That night I had a death wish and I wanted anyone to come up and try me.

"Okay. Another." He poured and slid the glass over.

"Ahh." I drank it down, feeling the slight burn go down my throat. It had been a while since I had drank anything, but it was the same old beast. Beautiful and destructive all at once.

"Another." I said.

"Listen, pal. I've already poured you three. Don't you think that's enough for a bit?"

"Did I ask you to stop? I said another. I'll tip you triple this time."

"Sure. No big deal." He said. This time he was eying me with caution. It was obvious I wasn't someone to fuck with.

Drink, slam, and ask for another. That was the ritual at hand, right. "Another."

"One more, champ. Then I want you out of my bar." He said, loosely pouring me another shot. "I mean it. Last one."

"I hear you." I mumbled and took the shot.

"Alright, time to go." He said. He wouldn't take his eye off me for one second.

"You always stare at your customers like that? I didn't come to cause any trouble. Just wanted to drink in peace."

"I stare at people who come into my establishment with negative emotions surrounding them. We get a lot of that here. If a man downs four shots in a row, I know he's going to bring me down with him. Got it? Now get the fuck out." He threw a pointed finger at the door, which actually made me break down in heavy laughter. He didn't scare me. No one did.

At this stage in the night, I was drunk off my head. Really, I just wanted to disappear. "Do you know who I am?" I asked him, headed for the door.

"You're my mother's uncle. No, I don't know who the fuck you are and I could give two shits. Out!"

"I'm Liam Conway. Number 18 and starting quarterback for the New England Patriots." I slipped and the rest of the bar couldn't help but cackle with laughter. I threw the door open and the wind hit my face unexpectedly.

"Bye-bye, Liam Conway!" Someone drunkenly yelled from their seat.

I walked until I found a lone liquor store. "Light at the end of the tunnel." I whispered to myself. Tonight was everything it ought to have chalked up to be. I bought a bottle of whisky and walked to the park nearby.

Sitting and drinking aimlessly, I wondered to myself, "How funny would it be if a cop walked by me right now?" I could lose my career. *All for the better*, I decided. Maybe then I could get her back. Maybe then I could have a real fucking life.

No. That wasn't going to happen. She wouldn't be coming back to this wreck. She was long gone and I simply had to accept it. But men like me don't accept the hard truth too easily. Men like me fight. We get maimed, shot, and lose limbs for the big things in life.

The night I met her – that man held a gun to our heads. I risked getting shot just to save her. Couldn't she see I loved her? Couldn't she understand that I would do anything for her? Shit, relationships are hard and people make mistakes. But if you really loved someone, shouldn't you give them more than one chance? I know I had done wrong. I know it. But I was willing to take a step in a new direction.

I fell asleep with that bottle in my hand. By the time my eyes closed it was empty and dry as a bone. Men like me didn't give up without a fight. Only problem was I was only fighting myself.

Laura

The TV in the bar blared loudly. I normally didn't go for mimosas this early, but I didn't have to shoot until eight PM, so why not? A sitter the network had suggested, thank God, was watching Alex. So it was me, all by myself. Just like old times. I could do anything I wanted. Of course, somehow I was sitting watching the fucking Patriots game in a bar in the Lower East Side of Manhattan.

"I'll take another, please." I said politely.

"Sure thing." The bar tender, classy and very put together, said.

The TV roared above us: "*And there we have it, folks! The Patriots, playing a good game this morning, but not good enough.*" The one announcer said.

Another chimed in, saying, "*One can only imagine what Liam Conway would have brought to the table.*"

The first commentator laughed, *"If you have just started tuning in, Liam is nowhere in sight. It looks like his half-game suspension is turning into a complete no-show..."*

The bar tender shook his head as he gave me my second mimosa. I took a sip and eyed him. "Why the shake of the head?" I asked.

"Where the hell is he?" He threw his hands up in the air.

"Who? Liam Conway? Aren't you in New York? You can't be a Patriots fan." I joked.

"I'm from Boston, born and raised. I'm just out here for this job. I'm banking on the Patriots winning the Super Bowl. He needs to be out there. They're shit without him."

"He's a bit reckless though, don't you think?" I asked him.

"Reckless? He's the best quarterback the world's ever fucking seen. So he got into a fight? Even the NFL doesn't give a shit about that."

"But he got suspended." I argued.

"Yeah, for half a game. I saw that. Doesn't mean shit. They have to do that kind of stuff. They know not to press him too hard though. They need him in there. He wins and he sells tickets. I just don't know where he is or what the hell he thinks he's doing by not showing up."

"Yeah, me too." I whispered. I grabbed my phone from my purse and decided to do the unexpected thing. I called him. "Can you excuse me for one second? I have a phone call to make."

"Sure thing, doll." The man winked at me as the phone rang into my ear.

Somewhere in Massachusetts, Liam answered his phone solemnly. "Yeah." He said.

"Liam? It's Laura…" I waited for a reaction. Anything to tell me he was at least okay. He disappointed me, but I still wanted the best for him.

"Laura? Hi, uh, Hey. How are you?" He sounded congested, like he was just waking up. Weird, however, was the fact that I could hear the sounds of people talking in the background.

"Where are you? What the hell are you doing?" I asked.

"Nothing, I... Nothing." He mumbled. The sounds of birds chirping and kids playing echoed in the background.

"Are you in a park?" I asked him.

"I went for a walk." He said. "What's going on? I thought you didn't want to speak to me anymore."

"I didn't say that. I just want you to recognize your mistakes. Anyway, that's a different conversation for a different time. You have a game to play, dammit!" The people next to me at the bar turned and looked at me.

The bar tender stopped drying one of his glasses and whispered, "Can't be him, can it?"

"I was suspended, remember? Besides, none of them want me out there. I'm a fucking joke. To everyone. I ain't worth jack shit." He said. "When the going gets tough, men like me get thrown into the gutter. It's not long after everyone forgets your name."

"Liam, you need to listen to me. Call a cab and have them take you to the stadium. Get a coffee, take a shower, and do whatever you need to do to wake the fuck up and play."

He shouted into the receiver, "No! I'm done with this game. You hear me? Done." At this point it was clear he was drunk. It was about an hour to halftime and if he didn't sober up fast he would lead his team into the ground.

"You idiot. Your team needs you. They're losing badly out there. If it's true that they hate you now, they won't when you lead them to victory. So sober up, you bastard, and take your team into the Championship game. We need a hero this morning." I said, hoping he'd come to his senses for once. The bartender had a huge smile on his face. He had stopped all his activities to listen to my conversation.

"You still done with me?" He asked me.

"We've already had this conversation. I definitely don't want to have it again. If you can't help yourself, then no one can. Not me, not your coaches, not anyone." I hung up the phone, furious at him once again. When would he learn that he needed to be strong without me? That was what I liked about him in the first place.

When we first got to know each other, it was as if everything changed in an instant. He was polite, strong, and clear-headed. Now he was losing it, falling asleep in parks and missing huge games. I couldn't even think about it. It was making me too angry.

"Was that…?" The bar tender gestured toward my phone.

"Yeah. We know each other. Long fucking story." I said, taking a big gulp of orange juice and champagne. "I'm going to need a third, please."

"Is he going to play? What happened? I can't believe you know Liam Conway!" He exclaimed for the whole bar to hear.

"Keep it down. I'd rather not let the whole bar in on my personal life." I said, motioning for him to speak quiet and close to me. "Who knows what he'll do." I shrugged.

"Fucking suspension…" The bar tender mumbled angrily.

* * *

Halftime came and went, and the Patriots were getting slaughtered to high hell. If I was on TV reporting on this, I would have said the team was done for. The morale was extremely low.

"Any hope for Liam Conway to save the day has now gone out the window. Folks, I think we know how this one ends."

I shook my head and pounded my fist on the table, drinking my fifth mimosa of the day. "Damn you Conway!" I yelled at the screen. "Bastard."

"Fuck the Patriots." Someone in a booth behind me said. I didn't even take a look to see who they were. I was glued to the screen.

"The Green Bay Packers are taking this one home. Another touchdown! I'm sorry to say it, but I don't see a light at the end of the tunnel for the Patriots. At this juncture, they need a miracle."

"Come on…" I whispered. "Don't let me down again." It was odd how invested I was in the game.

Liam and I may be done for good, but we would always be connected one way or another. I couldn't just watch as his team dug their own grave.

"Wait a second! Holy moly, folks! I can't believe my eyes. Is that…? Yes! It's Liam Conway!"

"Yes!" I screamed, jumping out of my seat.

"He ain't gonna do shit." Someone else yelled at the television. "Look at him. He looks like a wreck."

"Oh yeah? Is that what you think?" I turned around and faced them. "Just you watch."

Liam

"Conway is that you?" The crowd roared above me. They needed me, more than my team even, now more than ever. I threw my arms up in the air and ran to the coach.

"It's me." I mumbled. "Let's fuck these Packers up."

"You look like shit. I have half mind to send you back home. Where the hell were you?" His arms were crossed, his face strained. I could tell he was angry, but he also needed me.

"Out drinkin'." I smiled. I was at the end of my ropes. I didn't care anymore. I was going to win this game. End of story.

He pulled me in closer so that no camera could read our lips. "You come on my field and disrespect me like this? I've been there for you from the start, Conway, but this is fucking ridiculous. You're lucky as hell I need you right now. If I didn't, I'd send you home and recommend a permanent suspension." He spit onto the field below him.

"Don't worry, coach. I got this. Call him out." I pointed to the second-rate quarterback they had thrown in on a whim.

The coach blew his whistle and motioned for him to come in. The kid gave me a look of disgust and I whispered, "Watch how a real player does it." I ran out onto that field and never looked back.

In the huddle I came face to face with my demons. I looked everyone dead in the eye, one at a time, and took a sigh of relief. "It's good to be on this field. Now, I know you all hate me. For good reason probably. But now's not the time to go against me. We're down by 14 points. By my calculations, that's an easy fucking win. But you have to listen to me. You have to play ball. For the next few hours, are you with me? Will you stand next to me and lead these Packers to their graves?"

I looked around at the players. Charlie nodded. He said, "You're a son of a bitch, you know that?"

"Shit. I know it." I laughed.

"How many times are you going to come onto this field with apologies? We don't need apologies or pep talks or nothing. We need to win." Jimmy said.

"Then let's win." I smiled. "On three. Victory." Our hands fell into the middle, one on top of the other. We are all in this together.

1-2-3 VICTORY!

Our hands flew into the air. Before we knew it, we were out on that field, eyes in front of us, dodging the some of the hardest defensive players the NFL has got. Pass after pass, run after run, we began to gain solid ground once again.

The sports commentators were eating this shit up. *"I can't believe my eyes! Liam Conway, controversial as ever, is redefining what it means to be a football player. He is truly giving this game his all this morning."*

Fourth and long, we only had one real shot. I was still drunk, depressed, and angry, but when I got into the zone, there was no stopping me. *"HIKE!"* The ball came directly into my hands. I looked for

Charlie. No, he wasn't in the clear. Jimmy. Shit, it wasn't looking good.

Three linemen were barreling towards me. Everything moved in slow motion now. The sound had grown filtered and almost non-existent. One guy's hands were on my shoulders. I spun and broke free from his grasp. *Fuck*, I thought. Is this it? Is this what losing felt like?

I nearly fell to the field, losing my balance. But something kept me up on my toes. I decided my only chance was to make a run for it. I pushed one guy away from me, while ducking through the other's outstretched arms. It was like running through a firefight. I only had one narrow path and if I didn't make it, I would lose everything. They would take the ball and bring it to another touchdown.

Only 7 yards to go. I just needed that first down. One yard, two yard, three yard, four yards passed. One of the Packers wrapped his hands around my ankles. "No!" I screamed, dragging my feet. Another yard down. *Just stay up on your feet, dammit.* One more yard down.

Men were diving at me, coming from all angles. I was done for. I started to tumble, I reached my arms forward, and finally hit the ground. The crowd cheered above me. I tried to discern whether their cries were good or bad. I looked at the ball and then the referee, and it was called. I got my first down.

I threw my fist into the air ran back to the huddle. "Alright, second chance. Standard formation. Jimmy, you're going long. We're cutting into their lead once and for all." I said. He nodded. "Charlie, back me up out there. You'll be my bodyguard today." We broke the huddle and decided to go for it.

I dropped back, eyes on the target. Jimmy gave me a nod as he turns, so I threw the ball with about as much force and speed as a bullet launched from a pistol. The catch was direct and smooth. *Touchdown!* It was hard to find a defensive team that could compete with my throw.

I high fived my teammates and walked to the sidelines. Coach Stevens shook my hand and playfully slapped my ass. I jumped forward. "You did good out there."

"Yeah?" I unattached my helmet and ran my hands through my wet hair. "You don't want to take me out anymore? Sounds like a bad idea now don't it?"

"You're doin' good. Just bring it home." He said.

"Thanks coach."

* * *

The game went as planned. By dedicating ourselves to a strict wall of defense, as well as pushing strong offensive plays with the best players we had, we took the game home. Touchdown after touchdown. Throw by throw.

At the end of the game, I turned to look at the crowd. They were all just faces to me, every single one of them. Those faces chose to come out to see us win for their state, night after night. So far, we've lifted their expectations. So what do we get in return? Fast cars? Endless money and satisfaction?

I sat at the press conference after with that thought in mind. Laura. Most men would have given up by now. Something in me was pushing me to keep trying. Maybe I was deficient. Maybe I should have just let it go. Then again, that kind of thing wasn't for a guy like me. A real man keeps on fighting. A real man stands against the flames, despite the odds.

A reporter, some young graduate from Columbia, Harvard, or some other school of privilege, stood up and asked, "You had a rough start this season. What's changed inside of Liam Conway? What made you want to play better?" She listened attentively for my answer, notepad in hand.

"You mean besides wanting to win it all? The money? The cars? No, I'm joking. It's actually, uh, going to sound a bit cheesy. I met a girl worth fighting for. Unfortunately, we're not together anymore, but she gave me hope. She made me realize my love for the game just as it was starting to slip away." I said.

"Slip away? What do you mean by that?" She asked.

I scratched my head. It was embarrassing having a hundred microphones shoved in your face, waiting for your philosophical opinion on subjects you're barely qualified to answer. It's all a part of the game, I guess. I just hoped Laura was watching.

"It's as simple as it sounds. I hate to admit this, but after winning that Super Bowl last year, my love for the game was slipping away. I love playing, but there's all this other stuff surrounding the sport that really has no place on the field. Secretly, I was ready to give up, ready to throw in the towel and leave forever." Some of my teammates shuffled in their seats. One of the coaches coughed loudly. "Fuck it, I ain't afraid to speak my truth. This woman saved me. That's all. And now I'm giving all the remaining teams this warning: Watch your back. 'Cause I'm coming for you." The sounds of cameras clicking, laptop keyboards clacking, and smart phones bleeping could be heard all over the room.

Another reporter stood up and asked, "No fights today, huh?" I shrugged. I wasn't going to take the bait that easily. "I'm guessing the suspension made you think about what's at stake."

"You guessed wrong." I laughed and closed my eyes for a brief second. I had to decide how I would answer this one. "You know, there's a lot of tactics a player can use on the field to intimidate the other team. Using words is generally the weakest and easiest route to choose to do that." I stopped myself short and took a deep silence.

Laura

"Care to elaborate, Liam?"

At this point, I had left the bar and headed home. The press conference was on as I held Alex in my lap, sewing a pocket of his pants.

Liam smiled, giving the reporter that signature cocky look of his. "If one of the players fucked with me today out on the field, I would have pummeled him just like I pummeled that second-string loser last game. See, sometimes you guys with the cameras can't hear what is said out the field. Well, it just so happens that the guy I socked deserved it. That girl I love, the woman I mentioned earlier… He made a comment saying he was going to, well, he said he was going to do inappropriate things to her."

The whole press whispered loudly. I felt my stomach drop. He was defending me? *Shit...*

He continued speaking. The tone of his voice was sounding more humble by the second. "I just snapped. It's not that weird to blow up on the field. You in the press love it and the audience loves it too. This was different though. If a man is going to insult the woman I love, at least have the decency to say it to me when I'm on my feet. I'll still sock you in the teeth, but at least then it's a little fair to me." He laughed. "No but really, people laugh when I say this out loud, but I'm done with all that fighting shit. I'm not one of those guys who is into punching people in the face every game. But if you insult the mother of my child, you better fucking expect to end up in the hospital." He leaned back in his chair and said, "And one more thing…"

I hit the TV screen. "Oh, Liam…" He had a million excuses, but this time he actually sounded genuine.

Alex started to run around the house in excitement. "Liam! Liam!" He repeated, running in circles.

"Your dad is a jerk," I began, rolling on the floor next to Alex. I laughed. "And I can't believe I'm saying this, but I really love him. I really do."

Alex smiled, probably too young to understand the intricacies of love. Although, maybe not. Fact was, he and his dad were all I had left in my life as a constant. Even Katherine would someday leave me to pursue her own life and love. Liam was always there for me. Despite his character flaws, he had really changed into someone worth standing by. I couldn't believe he admitted to having a kid on national television. It wasn't exactly the best way to announce it, but it sure did make my cheeks grow hot with excitement.

"He was just protecting me. I thought he was reckless. I thought he was being selfish. I fought him hard. Oh, Alex. I think momma's made a big mistake." I said, chewing on my finger nails.

"Big mistake." Alex said back to me.

"I, uh," Liam continued, "I'd like to, uh, use this forum as a place to ask an important question. That is, if everyone is okay with that."

There was a slow rumbling of whispering voices. He ignored them and chose to continue speaking. "On the off chance that she's watching this on TV, there's something important I'd like to ask you. Laura, you're the love of my life. Since you met me I've been cocky, I've been shitty, and I've been downright irresponsible. But I *have* to tell you that that's not me. Deep down, I'm someone different. I'm honest, good, and trustworthy. I know that seems impossible now, but if you just give me another chance, I'll make it up to you tenfold. I love you, Laura. And, uh, will you...will you marry me?" The whole crowd of reporters and fans gasped.

"Who's the mystery girl Laura?" One reporter yelled out. Another screamed from the back while standing on a chair to be heard, "Marriage? What about your bad boy image?"

"Fuck my bad boy image! It was you who created it. Not me." He said, flipping the cameras off. "I'm out. See ya." And just like that, he walked out of the press conference.

I grabbed my purse and threw a change of clothes inside. "Come on, baby. We're going on a little trip to Massachusetts. It's time to get your dad back." Filming would have to wait.

* * *

Outside, it was raining and chaotic. The winds were picking up high speeds and the stop lights were shaking against the force of the earth's systems. A taxi cab stopped at the corner and its radio was blaring loudly out the man's window. *"We have a major storm hitting the city, as well as upstate New York. It is advised you stay indoors as winds are gaining speed at a rapid rate."*

"Taxi!" I yelled. The cabbie got out of the car, holding his hat on against the wind.

He opened the door for us, yelling above the sounds of thunder and rain, "Inside! Inside!" He ran back to his seat and slammed the door.

"Thanks for taking us. Can you do long-distance trips?" I asked, hoping he would say yes. It was worth a try. All of the trains had been shut down because of the storms and the thought of taking a huge bus in this storm with my baby was frightening to say the least.

"No long distance." The man said. "Only city."

"I'll pay you double. It's important." I pleaded with the man, showing him I had the cash to pay. "I need to get to the greater Boston area. Please."

"Not in this storm!" The cabbie exclaimed, throwing his hands into the air.

"I'll pay you triple." I said. "Trust me, I'm good for it."

The man leaned back against the seat, turning his head to face me. "What do you want to go to Boston for? It's rainin' cats and dogs out here and you got a baby in your arms. Is it really that important to you?"

"It is." I said. "It's more important than you know."

"You know, my wife and kids are out of town for the weekend. I don't really have nothin' to do and there ain't anybody waiting for a cab in the city today. Guess it's your lucky day, huh?" He put the cab in drive and sped against the wind.

"You're going to take us? Oh, thank you!" I exclaimed with glee. "You hear that Alex? We're going to see daddy!"

Liam

I walked down from the podium knowing full well it wasn't a good press conference. I had said too much. Too honest, they would tell me. At this point I was used to the whole shtick. I'd go to my agent's office, apologize, and then play a slew of games that'll make them forget the incident ever happened.

My coach cut me off on the way to my car. "The suits want to talk to you, Liam."

"Shit. They pissed about the press meeting? To be honest, I thought it went as well as it could. You know, considering the circumstances."

"Son, those men operate on a different wavelength from me. I have no idea what they want from you. All I know is they want to speak with you."

I grabbed my phone and called my agent. "You want to speak with me?"

His tone was light and excited, the exact opposite of what I was expecting. "Liam, sweetheart! How are you?"

I glanced at the dark clouds forming above the city and frowned slightly. "I've seen better days, but overall I'm good. I heard you needed to speak with me. What's up?"

"I just wanted to let you in on some of the calls I've been getting today…"

"Look, I just want to apologize about the press meeting. I know I got a problem with running my mouth, but I can't always be honest. I should have consulted you guys before announcing to the world I am in love and have a kid out of wedlock."

Though I thought I was going to get talked down to, the guy actually laughed when he heard me say that. "Are you kidding? Everybody loved that. First of all, everyone's had a kid out of wedlock. It's not a big deal and the fact that you actually care seems to boost your appeal quite a bit. People are losing their shit over this, Liam. And they're doing it in the best way possible." He said.

"Really? I guess honesty has its charm." I muttered back, sort of dumbfounded people even gave a shit about that sort of thing.

"Everyone is dying to know who this mystery woman is." He said.

"Yeah, well, it doesn't matter much. She's done with me now. It's time for me to move on." I solemnly admitted.

"No!" He shouted. "Liam, if there's one thing I know, it's that nothing is over until it is over. Find her. Reconcile your relationship dammit. Think about your career."

"She isn't some object. She's a woman and she has nothing to do with my career. You got to get that through your head. I don't give a fuck about your ratings or popularity charts. I throw my best and make good decisions out on that field. I lead my team to victory. That should be good enough for you."

I hung up the phone and smiled big. I was finally back to the point where I could be myself again. I ran further outside to my car and jumped in quickly. It was now pouring over the city of Boston and I was half-soaked. I was just about to pull out and head home when I heard someone yelling my name.

"Liam! Hey Conway!" The voice said. I turned and tried to look out the rain-soaked window. It was Jenkins!

"There's the man of the hour!" He said with a grin on his face.

"I saw you were playing a game in New York in a few days. I had no idea you'd be out here though! Why didn't you text me? Oh, by the way, congrats on winning those playoff games. That's huge. Can't believe we're both going to the Super Bowl. Hope you're prepared."

I unlocked the car and watched as he dove inside. "Man, it's deadly out there right now. I had a layover here, but they've cancelled all the remaining flights for the day. Anyway, I thought I'd come out and see you. Figured I'd just wait until this whole circus died down. You played good out there today by the way."

"Thanks man. Yeah, I never thought it would happen. Two blood-brothers, facing each other in the

Championships. You remember back in college when we made that pact?" I laughed.

He suddenly looked very nostalgic. "Yeah, man. I remember. We said we'd always back each other up. We will, right?" He asked me.

"Always." I said with pride. "You have to admit, it's plenty weird how the deck gets shuffled sometimes."

He nodded, licking his lips. "Man, I feel that. You know I love a good challenge." He wiped some of water off his Under Armor and got comfortable. "So what's this about marriage? You really serious about all that?" He asked me.

"The woman drives me crazy." I admitted. "Yeah, I'm serious."

"What about your old lifestyle? How do you plan to kick all those habits?" He laughed. "Imagine. Liam Conway without a multitude of pussy on him at all times! Man, that just seems wrong. It's like a dog without an owner."

I chuckled. "I'm not sure I get the analogy." I said. "I'm getting old Jenks. I'll be 33 next December. You know what that means, right?"

"Shit, don't even worry about nothing. You think they're going to force you out of the game?" He asked, sensing the reality of the situation. Jenkins was 28. He hadn't felt the entire weight of life yet. I suppose I hadn't either. "Wait, you're serious?"

"The average age of retirement in the NFL is 30, man. Who am I kidding? They've been tryin' to force me out for years. I've just been good at proving I'm still a great return of investment." I bit my lip and thought about it all for a second. It was a bullshit situation, but it was one I had chosen to live with. "So yeah, I love her. And someday soon, when I'm forced out, I'll run away with her and we'll never look back."

"Sounds like a perfect plan, but right now you have to keep focusing on the game. Look man, I came to talk to you about some actual serious shit." His smile turned into a dark frown. His muscles tensed up as the rain began pouring harder.

"Bad storm." I acknowledged, nodding my head at the rolling thunderclouds and lightning in the distance. "Alright, Jenkins. Give me the serious stuff."

"They don't want you to win that Super Bowl. In fact, they don't want you near it." He simply stated.

"Who doesn't?" I asked with a straight face. I ran my fingers across my stubble. I could have went for a drink right then and there had Jenkins wanted to soften the blow of the news. Instead, I sat there like an ill patient waiting to hear his death sentence.

"The networks. The investors. All the top mother fuckers. I overheard my agent and coaches talking the other day. They want our team to win it, not you guys."

I shook my head in complete disbelief. "That's not how it works, brother. It's not up to the networks or CEO's. It's up to the God damn players who win the games." My hand was wrapped tightly around the steering wheel, even though I was completely secure and stationary in park.

"You know as well as I do that's not how this shit works. They're paying the coaches extra to get there. They're telling them to put in certain players at certain times. You know, telling players to get injured and shit. It's all fucked up. They're coming up with ways to stop you from winning. They've got a lot riding on this game, you know." His face looked angry. His eyes had creased downward, while his lips were cracking from the stress.

"Yeah? So what? Let them try. The people will have their say. They want me in and I'll win it for them. My agent just said my popularity rating has shot up." I argued. I just didn't see how they would even be able to succeed at this, especially when nothing of the sort had been mentioned to me.

"Don't you understand? They're trying to get you barred from the rest of the last few games!" His expressions had grown volatile. He had expected me to overreact, perhaps punch a window or two, or maybe down a bottle of vodka or whisky. Instead, I sat calmly looking out at the incoming storm. It was oddly comforting to me right now.

"I guess I just don't believe it. I know they hate me and all. Everyone loves to hate me. That doesn't mean they're really going to get me barred. It doesn't mean that my team has to lose because of money. Shit, they tried to suspend me for a full game and failed at that!" I exclaimed with utter justification. It wasn't that I didn't believe him. I actually did. Jenkins was the most trustworthy guy in the game. The trouble was, I didn't *want* to believe him.

This time it was him who punched my dashboard. "That? That was just the beginning of the big setup. I'm telling you, they'll do *whatever* it takes to get you out of that game. If you are going to make a good case for yourself and get the public to adore you, you better start now." He said.

"Alright, I get it. I think I see what you're asking me to do." I nodded, still staring off into the horizon. My hands were ready to ring the necks of the network supervisors. Now that I knew what their plan was, I was going to do everything in my power to stop them. I was going to win game after game until we brought that Super Bowl trophy home to Massachusetts. *Fuck them*, I thought to myself.

"That's why I asked if you were serious about this marriage thing. 'Cause if you are, it's time reinvent how the public sees Liam Conway." His smile had come back on his face.

"You got it. I'm can't believe I'm about to say this, but… I'm calling Cindy."

Laura

"Daddy? Is that where I'm taking you to? The kid's dad? I, eh, don't mean to pry or nothin'. Just passing the time." The cab driver said. We were a couple hours into the drive and nearing Boston with each passing mile.

"It's okay, I don't mind." I smiled from the backseat. Alex was sound asleep, hanging over my lap like a lump of heavy bricks. "Me and the kid's father have sort of a complicated relationship." I loosely admitted.

"Yeah? I get it. Me and my first wife had something like that." He said.

I could tell he could really use the conversation so I took the bait. "What happened?" I asked him.

"Ah, she passed some time ago. Fucking lymphoma. Time catches up on all of us, right?" Upon hearing this, my stomach sank. The man continued to look at the road. "We're gonna hit this storm. Prepare for some wind and heavy rain, everybody." He said, straining his eyes to see. He adjusted his lights and pushed forward.

"I am so sorry for your loss." I whispered, unable to say really anything else. I couldn't imagine losing someone so close to me like that. It tore at my heart just thinking about it.

"It's alright. It's more tough on the kids, you know? They loved their mother." He shook his head and sighed quietly. The road was getting bumpier and Alex shook in his sleep.

I leaned forward, entranced by his story. "Yeah, but she was the person you fell in love with. You went through all those experiences with her and then she was gone. I can't imagine." I said. And then after some seconds of awkward silence I added, "I'm sorry. It's not my place to say anything more."

He laughed a big burly New Yorker type of laugh. "Hell, you can't offend me. I grew up on the streets of that big city. I've heard and seen much worse. But you're right. It was hard for me, but I also don't live in a storybook land. I know that people come and go. I know nothin' lasts forever. My kids though. Shit, they don't know that yet."

"Yeah. Children are innocent." I said, feeling light headed.

"You said you and your husband are going through some things?" He asked me.

"Boyfriend, not husband. Well, it's complicated, like I said. He didn't know I had his kid. He, uh, is a big sports player. We lost contact. It was a whole cluster-fuck of an ordeal. Well, still is actually." I gave a small awkward laugh and picked at the seams of my shirt.

"Sports? I'm a huge baseball fan. Does he bat?" He turned his head halfway around with a newly vested interest.

"No he throws." I said. And when he didn't understand what I was talking about, I reiterated. "Football. He's a quarterback. Liam Conway." I found myself saying his name aloud. Conway. The name rolled off my tongue like butter.

I missed him, despite all of our issues. I remembered his body, the heavy touch from his fingers and his strong grasp. He would envelop me with his arms, consume with his body and massive cock. After fucking him, I would lay in bed suffocating from a lack of air and energy. I wanted to feel that way again. I wanted to feel his obsession wash over me.

I felt my legs tingle with anticipation. Just the thought of his gaze set me off. The cabbie, however, interrupted my train of thought. "Liam Conway? You're kidding! You're going to get *that* son of a bitch back? Never mind, honey! I take it all back. Let's turn around now!"

"Not a big Patriots fan, I take it?" I laughed slightly.

"Hell no!" He yelled, nearly waking Alex up. "Listen up, I'm from Brooklyn. Born and raised. *Fuck* the Patriots!" He cackled out the window, speeding through branches and other debris from the storm.

I laughed and said, "Yeah, well, I think all sports are kind of goofy. A bunch of greasy men touching each other? It's kind of weird. And I hate the violence of the sport, you know?" I thought about what I had just said and decided to correct myself. "Okay, the men touching each other. That can stay. The rest I couldn't care less about."

"So you're the one he was talkin' about at the press conference weren't you. *Shit*!" He swerved to the side of the road to avoid a massive tree right in the middle of the freeway. "Sorry about that folks, it's getting scary out there. Better put on your seat belts."

He zipped around the rubble and made his way onto the road once more. *Almost there*, I thought. *Just a half hour left.* With all the shaking from the drive, Alex had woke up frightened.

"Daddy?" He said, looking around the cab.

"I ain't your daddy." The cab driver laughed.

"That was me he was talking about. He's crazy." I said.

"Ha! I'll bet you a million bucks it's also the reason why you love him."

I couldn't help but nod in agreement. It was true. I loved him because of who he was. He was talented, strong, deep, and he was also a reckless asshole.

"Say no more. I'll get you to him in no time!" He slammed his foot into the pedal, laughing as the big lug of metal pushed through the storm.

* * *

Finally, we reached the freeway entrance to the city. Most players lived outside of Boston, but of course Liam had to do things his way. Liam liked living in the city, amongst all those big buildings, despite him being very vocal about hating it. We pulled up to a long series of luxury condos and stopped. The engine was idling and the sound of rain tapping against the aluminum ricocheted around us.

"We're here." Our driver said. He turned to look at me and said, "No being sad or angry, or any of those other negative emotions. You're a strong woman, you hear me? You'll be a great family someday. Just listen to him. Hear him out. You'll figure it out together. I know you will."

"I'll try." I said, fondling a wad of cash in my purse.

He waved my hand away. "No need. Just give me an even $60 and we'll call it a day."

"You serious?" I asked him, grabbing three 20's from my wallet.

"I just want to see you two flourish. I'll be watching the TV for updates!" He laughed and honked the horn. "Alright, out of my cab. Both of you!"

I jumped out, holding Alex and running to the nearest outside ceiling. I was soaked from head to toe and so was Alex, though he was remarkably calm. I called Liam and he answered almost immediately. "Hey, is everything alright?" He asked me. I could hear the same thunder in the background of his phone.

"Are you home?" I said, wiping the rain from my eyes.

"Yeah. Wait, why? What's going on?"

"What floor?" I asked him, ignoring the question.

"Third floor. Room 32. Can you tell me what the hell is going on?" He asked me.

"Nothing. Everything is fine." I said, hanging up the phone. I ran up his staircase and found door

number 32. I knocked carefully and waited for my
man.

Liam

"Laura?" There she was, in all her beauty, the love of my God damn life.

"Hi Liam." She whispered, shivering and covered in rain and leaves. Alex coughed from the cold wind outside.

"Come in! Sorry, I would've cleaned if I knew someone was coming." Beer cans were littered across the floor. Clothes were everywhere. It was all to be expected when you went through a breakdown like I did.

I grabbed Alex gently from her arms and kissed his forehead. He felt cold. "We should run him a warm bath. I don't want him getting sick." I said. "I'll heat up some milk from the fridge."

I bundled him up in a fresh towel and set him on the coach. I then ran into the bathroom and began running a warm bath for him. "Thank you." Laura said from the living room.

"It's no thing. Really. I'm happy to do it." I said. I made sure the water was at a good temperature. Once the water got to a good level, I stopped it short and settled Alex into the water. He simply smiled the whole time, completely calm and happy to be alive.

Laura placed her hip against the bathroom door and watched as I began playing with him from the outside of the bath. There wasn't much, but I *did* have some old toys from when I was a kid hidden away in a drawer off to the side. I grabbed an old plastic boat and placed it in the water. He instantly took a liking to it, splashing water at the little tugboat.

"There you go!" I said enthusiastically.

"Can we talk for a second?" Laura asked me suddenly. Her voice sounded as if it had a slight tinge of sadness to it.

"Yeah, of course. But before you say anything, I just want to say that I'm sorry and I've thought it all through. I'm okay with it now." I said. "You know, I wasn't before, but now I think I am." But I wasn't acting normal and both her and Alex could sense it almost straightaway.

"Then why do you sound so weird?" She asked me. Then she moved a little closer to me and sat down. "Something tells me you're not okay with the way things are." She put her hand on my thigh suddenly.

"I…" I tried to speak, but she cut me off before I could get a word in.

She held a finger up to my mouth. "Shh. It's okay. I'm not either. At least I think I'm not. I was wrong. Wrong about everything." She said.

I couldn't hold back my confusion. None of this made any God damn sense. "Excuse me? Is this for real?" I waited for Alex to pinch me so I could wake up from this fantasy, but he didn't. This was real alright. She was coming back to me.

"It's real. I'm real. You're real! And I need to stop pretending I don't love how insane you are." She said, now holding my face. I kissed her as fast and hard as I could.

"I've been praying to hear you say those words. Did you see the press conference? I want you forever, Laura Alvaroy. I want to raise our boy together. I want to support you and to watch your career blossom. Shit, I want to put another baby in that basket and I want to be the best fucking father on this planet. If you just give me a chance I'm changing everyday and I'm changing fast. I promise you. This time I won't let you down." I said, exhausted from letting out all I had held in. I stared at her, waiting for a response. Anything, I just wanted to hear her speak again.

"Just promise me you'll win this Super Bowl. Okay?" A short smile came jutting across her cute face.

"My brown eyed girl." I whispered, feeling her soft hair between my fingers once again.

"Like the song." She whispered back, getting closer to me.

"I always loved that song. I love you even more though." I said to her. But reality came and hit me like a ton of bricks.

I looked at her gorgeous face, only I was troubled now. "They want me out of the game, Laura. I don't know what to do."

"They want who out of the game? You? Like hell they do!" She exclaimed. Alex splashed around in the water more, upon hearing this.

"I'm serious. I saw Jenkins today. He's got word the networks think I'm too irresponsible to bank on. My record has been too shaky this past season and now I'm fucking 33 years old, three years older than the average player in the whole league. I'm telling you, they want me to fail."

"Liam, why would they want you to fail? I just don't get it." She said, draining the bath tub for me. I quickly grabbed a clean towel and wrapped Alex up in it, rubbing his hair dry. Someday he'd be my age and I prayed he wouldn't have to deal with any of this bullshit. He'd be a doctor, or a lawyer, or just a regular working guy who owned a house on the shore of San Diego. Anything but a ball player.

"I don't know, Laura. I really don't. It's like I said. Maybe because I'm too reckless. I wasn't playing well until I got to the playoffs."

"I need to make a few calls." She said, drying her hands off and walking out of the bathroom. Her heels clicked against the smooth tile floors.

"Laura, don't." I said, but it was too late. She was on the balcony making a call to her network to get some information out of them.

Outside, I could see her throwing her hands up wildly, arguing into the phone. I couldn't make out the words, so me and Alex just sat staring at her with confused looks on our faces. Finally, after a few minutes, she walked back inside and shut the sliding glass doors.

"Someone is lying to you." She simply said.

"What do you mean *someone* is lying to me?" I asked her, picking myself up off the couch in the living room.

"I mean, either Jenkins is lying or someone is lying to him. I don't know who the hell is, but *someone* is! I just called Jacob and he said nothing like that is going on. They're all banking on you winning. The networks, the ad agencies, fucking

Wheaties. They all want you to win this, Liam." She stood in front of me, arms crossed.

"What're you saying, Laura? You really think Jenkins wasn't telling me the truth? I've known him forever. We made a pact together. We promised each other we'd always be there for each other. Why would he do that to me?" I said, justifying everything. I don't know why I was fighting it so hard. This industry was cut-throat and I knew Jenkins had the drive to win. Maybe she was right.

"Isn't it obvious? He wants to get into your head, Liam. He wants you to lose. For Christ sakes, he's on the opposing side now. There can only be one winner, right?" She looked at me as if I needed some waking up to do.

"Holy…" I whispered. "Are you thinking what I'm thinking?"

Her eyes widened. "Holy shit. It was Jenkins who went to the Enquirer and told them you were seeing Cindy again. He knew it would cause controversy and hoped it would bleed into your skills out on the field!" She exclaimed.

"Laura, I called her today. When I met with Jenkins I called her up to run a piece in her magazine on the new Liam Conway." I bit down hard and felt my temperature begin to rise.

"The new what?"

"You know, a rebranding for my image. Nice guy Liam Conway. I was going to get rid of the whole bad boy image."

"He's making you look weak, Liam. You run that piece tomorrow and come Sunday you'll look like an old man who's tired of the game. Not only that, but how's it going to look to the rest of the world when you're seen with Cindy again?"

"But—"

"No buts about it. I appreciate the gesture, trust me. But you don't want to do this. When were you supposed to meet with her?" She asked me as she dressed Alex in some new clothes. He was making noises, laughing to himself. I appreciated his light hearted vibe, but now was not the time.

"Now. I was supposed to be there now." I said, feeling frantic.

"Alright. Well, you dug your own grave. Now we have to offset this thing. Call your driver. I'm coming with you."

* * *

"I cannot believe you called me! I just *can't*!" Cindy squealed excitedly. She ran like a goose toward me, nearly falling over in her stilettos and black dress. As she hugged me, she turned her head to look at Laura. "Hello." She said out of spite.

"Believe it." I said. "But don't get used to me doing this. This is the last time." A makeup artist was preparing my face for the photo shoot.

"Oh, I do *not* think that's true. You've always been infatuated with me, Liam." Her brows were raised, along with her chin. She loved to try and bare the look of sophistication. Only, she wasn't sophisticated. She was sloppy and embarrassing.

Laura couldn't help but shake her head. She said, "Look, Cindy, we didn't come here to play catch-up. I get that you're obsessed with my boyfriend and father of my child, but we need this to go to print as fast as possible."

Cindy gave a loud sigh and yelled, "Can someone get me a martini, God dammit?!" Then she turned to both of us and smiled, "Of course! Let's get started. You said you want to transform your image?"

Laura chuckled loudly. "Not exactly. We need you to run a piece on how he's going to win the Championships again. Talk about his stats. Talk about his and Jenkins' history together. Present it as the 'showdown of the century'. People love that sort of thing."

"Sounds easy enough." She smirked.

"Make me look as bad as I really am." I said. "Talk about all the trouble I've gotten in. All those fights, I'm a loose cannon. And yet, I'm bringing New England back to the Championships for one incredible game."

"And your agent is okay with all of this? I don't want to get a call at four in the morning from some coked out asshole asking me how I had the audacity to run this piece without him approving it."

"They'll be fine. At this point, it doesn't matter what I do as long as I win." I said.

"That's right, baby. You're *hot* right now."
Laura said, coming up behind me and kissing my
neck. Goosebumps shot through my body.

"You two make me sick." Cindy said. "Okay,
we'll get some shots taken. We'll need a few quotes
from you. Send us those stats too. I have to say, Liam,
Jenkins will not be happy about all this."

"Good. I'm slowly burying him in his own
grave."

Laura

"This is where it all takes place." He said to me, arms stretched out wide and eyes closed. It was as if he was living the glory of winning the game right now.

I sat in the front row of the empty bleachers. Alex, luckily, was with an expensive sitter, provided by the Patriots themselves.

"I can't believe you snuck me in here." I said.

"I can't believe you you're even here. Come here." He said to me. I got up and walked toward him. "Look." He pointed up at the giant screen.

"What? The screen? It's off." I said to him.

It suddenly turned on. "You never answered me." He said. The lights also turned on, one by one. Music started to play. It was the song "Brown Eyed Girl."

When I had turned to look at him, he was on one knee. In his hand was a giant diamond ring, delicately resting in a black box. "Laura." He smiled. Tears fell from my eyes instantly. I was so shocked. "Ever since I met you, my life has changed for the better. You've taught me how to be a better man, shown me how to grow as an individual, and made me realize that love is reality. We've had our ups and our downs. You've seen the worst of me, while always giving me the very best. And then there's Alex. Never in my life did I think I would make a good father. But now, after seeing the little guy, I know that my destiny in this life is to be there for both you and him. I just have one small question to ask you. Will you, Laura Alvaroy, be my wife? Will you marry me?"

I clasped my hands around my mouth. I fell to the AstroTurf and wrapped my arms around his muscular body. *Will you marry me?* "God, yes! Of course I'll marry you. You're the best and worst thing that's ever happened to me." I laughed, even though I was completely choking up on that field.

"Let's see how it fits." He said, quietly. I quickly wiped my tears away and extended my hand out. It was a perfect fit.

"I can't believe it. I'm going to be Mrs. Conway. That makes me the baddest woman in town, right?"

"So I see you've read the article already." He said with a sly smile on his face.

"It was wonderful, darling." I started to mimic Cindy's obnoxious voice. "Jenkins will not stand a chance out there."

"Ha! I can just see his face now. He's probably ripping his copy to shreds. I can't wait to face him on the field tomorrow."

"You're going to be so great, Liam. You always are." I said, leaning my face against his warm chest. I then slowly looked up at him. It wasn't long before he knew what was on my mind.

"You know," he began saying, "It's just us in here until practice. Now that you're my girl…" He gestured to his shorts. An indent was slowly forming around his growing cock.

"It's been too long." I said as he pushed my head downward into his lap. I pushed the back of my dress up so that my ass was exposed. "Finger me while I swallow that cock."

"You're perfect." He said to me. "You're an angel from heaven." He ran his hands down the middle of my back, across my spine, until he felt my cheeks. He lightly gave them each a slap and they bounced up and down.

I reached inside the legging of his shorts, realizing he wasn't wearing any underwear. His cock had already grown to an immense size. I slowly ran my fingers over the erect and veiny cock and lightly lapped on his balls with my tongue. Pushing three fingers together, he massaged the folds of my aching pussy, every so often inserting a finger or two inside.

Our sex that morning was adoring, impassioned, and perfect as ever. We hadn't been together like this in some time and because we were married, it was a reintroduction of sorts. It was like we had just met again.

As he was thrusting himself inside of me, I grabbed onto his hand with mine. My ring was reflecting off the lights of the stadium. Shining in my pupils was the reflection of his strong body, pushing in and out, closer than ever.

I held his hands tight, kissing and licking his fingers as he moved them across my tongue. He was here. He was really here. I wondered if he was thinking the same thing. There was so much push and pull to our relationship that when it finally was fixed, it felt completely surreal and beautiful. I gasped and moaned. He grabbed and groaned. Together, we connected in a way I had never experienced more. By the end of it, we were covered in our own sweat, unable to move. We just sat there, breathing deeply, feeling every ounce of pleasure move through our bodies.

We sat in the middle of the field now, holding each other. "I wonder if any of the players tomorrow will know your cum has fallen on the field." I joked, running my hands across his chest and perfect abs.

"Oh, God." He grunted. "That is hilarious. Not only am I going to beat them tomorrow. I'm also going to tackle them where my cum landed."

I playfully smacked his arm. "Gross!" I exclaimed.

"Hey, you started it." He said.

Then I realized what time it was. He would have to practice before the big game tomorrow. And tomorrow, he would he have to prove himself, a million times over, that he was still the best football player in the league. I believed in him, no matter how difficult the pressure was for him. I felt my gaze turn serious.

"Just promise me you'll be careful out there, okay? I don't want Alex to have to visit his injured dad in the hospital."

He looked at me with all the love in the world. "I promise you, whatever happens, I'm going to win that game. And right after I do, we're getting married. And it's going to be the best damn marriage anyone's ever laid eyes on. Alex will be the cutest ring bearer in the world." He said. He kissed my lips and then my cheek. "I'm never leaving your side. No injuries, no nothing."

Liam

The Championship game had finally arrived and Liam "The Shooter" Conway ran onto that field like a fucking cannon. I was about to win this game like a true baller, despite what the odds said about us winning.

Coach Stevens had told us at least four times that the bookies had all their money set against us. In their eyes, Jenkins was the one who was going to bring it on home, not me. Well, I hated to be the one who spoiled the party, but I knew in my gut that I had this in the bag.

But the feeling was bittersweet. When I looked into the crowd, Laura was there with Alex, eating their hot dogs. I wanted to throw the ball onto the grass and run into their arms. I wanted to leave it all behind. Football just didn't compare to shit. But there was a lot riding on this game. I knew that much at least. I gave Alex a thumbs up as I threw the first touchdown pass.

In the crowd were fans of all sorts. Faces I had never seen before were boo'ing me and telling me I should go to hell, while others were screaming about how they wanted to bear my children. It was a weird thing to experience. All of it, I had learned to tune out. It was here, on this field, where the scouts decided if I was still worthy of playing the sport.

The game, fortunately for the networks, was already close as hell. Jenkins, was bringing his A game to the table. I'd throw a scoring pass, and Jenkins would run out onto that field minutes later and catch one deep inside the end zone. It was fucking ridiculous.

Luckily, our defensive line was getting charged up and ready to go. After a quick pep-talk from the coach, they shouted the team name and ran onto the field, determined to defend our turf. Laura was watching intensely with a worried look on her face.

On the side of the field I looked at my phone. I had hidden it in a towel underneath the bench. I texted Laura: "Don't worry, baby. I'm about to win this game for you."

She glanced at me and smiled. Although, I could instantly tell something huge was weighing on her. "What's wrong?" I texted her.

After a few minutes, I got the text back. "I'm pregnant. Again." She said.

My jaw dropped.

"Conway! What're you doing?" I quickly hid the phone in the towel and shot up from the bench. "Get out onto that field!" Coach Stevens screamed at me. I looked out on the field and saw my offensive team waiting for me.

Shit, I muttered, running out to them. From the other side, Jenkins was shaking his head. He pointed at me and ran his index finger across his neck. Just my luck. I had to deal with women *and* friendship shit during the Championship game.

"Alright. Wishbone formation. This is a running play. I'll hand it to Randy and the rest of you are his defense. Got it? You guys ready?" The team nodded at me. There were no gimmicks this game.

There was only real leadership that worked. We were going to win this the old school way. "Alright. Break!"

I walked to my place, extending my hands outward. I couldn't stop glancing at Laura. I wanted to know that I was happier than ever. I wanted to tell her that it's what I've wanted to happen since we got back together in Los Angeles. "Hike!" I screamed. The ball spiraled into my hands and I dropped back and pivoted to the right.

Randy, who was moving like a salamander, stealthily grabbed the ball from my hands and ran seven full yards before being tackled. "Yes!" I hissed, slamming my fist into the air. Only three yards to go before we got a first down. I snuck a glance at Jenkins and began laughing to myself.

He pounded his fists against his helmet with rage. *What a clown*, I thought. I flipped him off and he came barreling onto the field like a ton of bricks.

He pushed his chest onto mine and said, "You want to fucking go, playboy?"

I pushed him off me, flexing my muscles and tightening my fist. If he really wanted to fight me, I was game. But he needed to remember one thing: "We had a pact, brother. Now what do we have?"

"You threw that away when you decided to slow down and throw away your football career for that stupid fucking woman." He cried out, getting angrier by the second.

"Say it. Say the words. I dare you. She means everything to me. She's worth more than the game. Shit, the game doesn't even come close." I spit.

"Yeah? And what about me? I guess our friendship meant nothing to you?" He ran his hands through his hair as sweat dripped down from his face. Security had rushed onto the field, pulling him off me.

"It's fine, I'm all good. Let him go. He'll cool off on the side of the field." I said to them. "Man, you're looking crazier and crazier by the second, making up lies like that to me. I should've known your ego was bigger than us. I just can't wait to keep winning out here today and put you in your place."

For the first time in my life, I walked away from a fight. It just wasn't the hassle. We brought it back in. I said, "Good running, Randy. You're killing it out there. Let's keep it short and sweet. All we need right now is three more yards and we get that first down. From there, we'll play hardball. This is a simple run and gun play, okay? Same as before, only this time I'll run it in."

"You?" Charlie interjected. "You sure? They're playin' tough out there. What if they sack you and we lose some yards?"

"We'll be fine." I said, unable to give him the time of day. As selfish as it was, I was going to be the star of the game. I just found out I was going to be a daddy, again, and I wanted to win this game for him. Or her, rather. "Alright, break."

As we ran back into the center of the field, Charlie whispered to me, "Stop taunting Jenkins. I know you guys have some shit to take care of between you, but don't even acknowledge him, man. Let's win this thing, make some money, and go home."

"I like where your head's at man." I gave him a hug and a pound and fell into formation. "Hike!" I grabbed the ball and attempted to run left. In my sight was a path to victory, an open and narrow road where no defensive lineman currently stood. Three yards was all I needed.

I ran at full speed, only I missed something important. One of the linemen had broken through the barrier to the right. He was blitzing me! "Fuck!" I yelled, only it was far too late. I dropped back, twisting my ankles together, as the lineman shot his head into my ribs. We came crashing down like two heavy weights and I instantly felt something tear. I heard it first, and then the pain radiated through my legs and body.

"No!" I screamed, clutching at my ankle. I must've torn my Achilles' Heel. I didn't know what else it could be. Laura, of course, came darting out of her seat. She was held back by security, forced to watch as a medic ran onto the field.

"Everything is fine." I yelled. "Just leave me alone. I'll be good in a few minutes." I lied.

The medic looked me square in the eye and reasoned with me. "Do you hear what you're saying to me? 'Cause what I'm hearing is that you don't care if you can walk on that knee ever again. It's pretty obvious you've injured yourself pretty bad."

"I'll sit for a few plays, but I am *not* letting that team go home with the trophy. Tell the coaches I'm fine and need some rest. If you don't, you'll regret it. And yes, that's a fucking threat." I muttered through my teeth.

The medic looked around and called it. "Pull him out for a few plays. He just needs to rest it off." He lied to the coaches. I thanked God he made that call.

Jenkins, however, was now screaming bloody murder on the side of the field. He just couldn't understand the call.

I sat on the side, twiddling my thumbs and feeling anxious. We had become too predictable now. Each play the coach called was met with hard defense and strong determination. By the time I was able to go back in, they had scored two touchdowns on us.

Before I ran back in, I checked my phone. "I'm so grateful for your love." She texted me. "I'm hoping you're not as injured as it seems. You need to give them all you got out there." I nodded and made my way onto the field. There was no stopping me.

Despite my urge to be the star of the game, I quickly realized we needed the whole team playing their best. It wasn't about me anymore, it was about the Patriots.

"Fuck it." I said to myself, picking a set of plays that could take us to the winning side. They were the back-up plays and they hadn't been used all season. I ran them, over and over again like heavy artillery during warfare. They didn't stand a chance. *Touchdown!* Charlie's hands wrapped around that pigskin and ducked into the end zone. That was one goal.

Lucky for us, my teammates recognized all that was at stake now. "You ready to play some ball?" I asked them. "That's right!" They screamed at the top of their lungs, "Patriots!" The cheerleaders were going wild and the audience was on the edge of their seats. Our defense held strong and forced them to turnover the ball back to us. With less than fifteen minutes left in the game, we had our work cut out for us.

We had those winning plays in our back pocket though, and as soon as I looked over at Laura, I know we'd win it. "Hut! Hut! Hike!"

I dropped back, knowing this was it, and eyed Charlie. "Come on, man. Take it home." I whispered. The ball left my hand like a bullet shooting through space. One of the linebackers tried to intercept the ball. It hit his palm and then his fingers, and for a split second I thought he had this. But even though it slowed down in speed and direction, Charlie caught the damn thing, running it into the end zone with seconds to spare. We had won the game. Tonight, Charlie was our man.

"You did it!" People cried out to him. Our team rushed the field and picked him up on their shoulders. The ice water was poured over Coach Stevens' back. Jenkins fell to the ground, pounding at the grass and crying like a little baby. As for me, I turned away from the team to find someone important to me, Laura.

Cameras flashed all around me, a reporter shoved his microphone in my face, but I swatted it out of the way. I jumped over the guardrail and ran up the bleachers. Fans from all over were running their hands over my pads, screaming for a picture. I ignored them. The game was over and I didn't care to bask in the glory of winning. Not to mention, my ankle was killing me.

I picked up my child and kissed his forehead. "You did it, Daddy!" He cheered. I wrapped my arm around Laura's waist and gave her the biggest kiss in the world.

The same reporter ran up behind me. He called out, "Liam Conway. You just won another Super Bowl! What do you have to say to your fans?" He asked me.

I turned to him and said, "I couldn't have done it without their support." The fans loved that kind of shit. "Wait. Scratch that. I couldn't have done it without *her* support." I corrected myself.

A million more questions flashed my way. Eager fans jumped around me. "That's all for tonight, guys. I have to make love to my fiancé. We're having another baby!" I screamed, picking both Alex and Laura up and running out of the stadium.

"Don't you have to be with your team?" She asked me as we fell into my car.

"Baby, there's nothing I'd rather do than be with you right now. Let's get out of this city. Let's take a trip." I said.

"A trip? Liam, you have to go to the after party tonight! There might be drafting scouts there." She practically screamed.

"Fuck all that." I said. Alex laughed and Laura gave me a scowl. "I'm serious, baby. Let's get out of here and start a life together. I've got all the money in the world. Let me spend it on my family."

She shook her head. "Okay. We can take a trip. But you're healing that leg and playing next season!"

"Fine. Whatever it takes to have your heart." I said, gazing into her eyes.

She sighed and gave me a longing look. "Oh, Liam. You had me from the beginning. I love you for finding me again."

That night we stayed up listening to music, cooking good food, and watching movies. We had missed out on so many things that couples do that we had to rush to play catch up. Despite it all, we both felt incredibly lucky. Whatever after parties were happening tonight, I was celebrating getting my family back. It was obvious we were meant for each other.

About the Author

Kara Hart is a new author from the Southwest. She's a full time student, writer, and mother of two loving dogs. She loves bad boys with a darker, sweeter side to them.

She knows someday she'll get invited into the MC...someday...

I LOVE hearing from my fans! I do my best to respond to everyone, so please follow me on Facebook.

If you're reading from a Kindle and would rather just type into your phone, I am authorkarahart on Facebook. Thanks again!

Other Bad Boy Books by Kara Hart!

[Image: Rust1.jpg]

[Image: image2.jpeg]

[Image: image3.jpeg]

Made in the USA
Middletown, DE
02 March 2017